## "Let's get a few things straight, shall we?

"I made a promise to a little boy, and I never back out on a promise. Not. Ever. My word is solid. Golden. Unaffected by time, distance or a change in circumstances."

Sutton sensed they weren't talking about Toby or the Soap Box Derby anymore. Casey's tone was too fierce, his expression too intense, his words too pointed.

"I like Toby. He's a great kid. I also like building cars. I'm good at it. Your son and I are going to have a lot of fun. It's really that simple, Sutton. Don't make this more complicated than it needs to be."

He was right. About all of it. She was overthinking the situation. But in this instance, she'd gone too far, and now she felt ridiculous and defensive. Should she apologize? Maybe lighten the mood?

Definitely the latter. "Well, I guess you told me."

"I guess I did." He cracked a smile, the boyish one that included the infamous head tilt, and just like that the tension between them was replaced by something far more potent.

**Renee Ryan** grew up in a Florida beach town where she learned to surf, sort of. With a degree from FSU, she explored career opportunities at a Florida theme park and a modeling agency and even taught high school economics. She currently lives with her husband in Wisconsin, and many have mistaken their overweight cat for a small bear. You may contact Renee at reneeryan.com, on Facebook or on Twitter, @reneeryanbooks.

### Books by Renee Ryan

### Love Inspired

#### *Thunder Ridge*

*Surprise Christmas Family*
*The Sheriff's Promise*
*Opening His Holiday Heart*

#### *Village Green*

*Claiming the Doctor's Heart*
*The Doctor's Christmas Wish*

### Love Inspired Trade

*The Widows of Champagne*

### Love Inspired Historical

#### *Charity House*

*The Marshal Takes a Bride*
*Hannah's Beau*

Visit the Author Profile page at LoveInspired.com for more titles.

# Opening His Holiday Heart

## Renee Ryan

**LOVE INSPIRED**
INSPIRATIONAL ROMANCE

# LOVE INSPIRED®

## INSPIRATIONAL ROMANCE

ISBN-13: 978-1-335-56740-6

Opening His Holiday Heart

This edition published by arrangement with Harlequin Books S.A.

For questions and comments about the quality of this book, please contact us at CustomerService@Harlequin.com.

Love Inspired
22 Adelaide St. West, 40th Floor
Toronto, Ontario M5H 4E3, Canada
www.LoveInspired.com

**Printed in U.S.A.**

Recycling programs for this product may not exist in your area.

Now faith is the substance of things hoped for,
the evidence of things not seen.
—*Hebrews* 11:1

For Bill and Sharon, my lifesavers,
and two of the best people I know.
I'm proud to call you brother and sister.

# *Chapter One*

Casey Evans sat in his vintage 1965 pickup truck, silently embracing the nickname his sister had given him—Ebenezer Grinch. Leave it to Remy to mix her metaphors with supreme accuracy. Casey did have issues with Christmas. Not that he would admit it out loud. To do so would lead to questions, which would require answers, and…nope. A man should be allowed his secrets, even from his family.

*Especially* from his family.

Apparently, Casey was the lone Ebenezer Grinch in town.

The sun had barely risen, the sky a faded pink against pale gray, but on this, the busiest shopping day of the year, Main Street was teeming with activity. As a business owner, he knew this was a good thing. In fact, Casey's coffee shop already had a line snaking out of the building.

Yet he couldn't quite make the leap from irritation to gratitude. It was the impromptu singing. All that paying homage to a Christmas tree and the *fa-la-la-la-ing*. Or maybe it was the miles of decorations his fellow business owners had already put up.

Stubbornly setting his jaw, he climbed out of his truck and, with an audible gulp, confronted the festive chaos. Hands on hips, feet spread, he took a good long look at what had once been a pleasant small town nestled in the Colorado Rockies. Not anymore. Thunder Ridge had turned itself into a Norman Rockwell painting. Literally. The town's new mayor had recreated one of the painter's famous Christmas scenes in the center of town. A virtual winter wonderland of lights, vintage cars and, of course, snow.

Ebenezer Grinch did not approve.

Time to get moving. Casey had a business to run. Employees to assist. "Bah, humbugs" to swallow. With his booted feet crunching on the freshly fallen snow, he elbowed his way through the crowded sidewalk, mumbling a series of "Mornin's" and "Excuse mes," while also fielding a barrage of return salutations. He got at least seven greetings of "Morning, Casey." A good ten shouts of "Merry Christmas, Casey." And a dozen variations of "Doesn't our town look festive?" along with "We're going to win that magazine contest, no question."

Sprinkled among all these cheerful predictions was the inevitable "Hey, Casey, how come you haven't decorated your coffee shop yet?"

He gave his stock response with a practiced shrug. "Too busy."

Not a complete lie. He was a busy man. Cargo Coffee wasn't the only business he owned. He had another location in a neighboring town and his fledgling airfreight company was, in a word, booming. Still, it was with great relief that he stepped into the scent of brewing coffee, yeasty baked goods, and…more singing.

It was going to be A. Day.

He spent the next few minutes settling in and trying to determine where he'd be the most useful. Seeing the frazzled duo at the espresso machine, he joined the mayhem there. The morning flew by. During a lull between the breakfast and lunch crowds, he restocked the bakery cases and then moved on to the display tables near the wall of windows overlooking the town square.

That was when he saw her.

Sutton Wentworth. Thunder Ridge's illustrious mayor. Widow, single mother, and Casey's personal nemesis since the "incident" back in high school. The one that had changed the direction of his life, that of his best friend, and, by default, Sutton's, as well. A thirty-four-year-old man did not hold grudges. And so Casey didn't. Most days. Really. Almost never.

He could not say the same about Sutton.

Ever since she'd moved back to Thunder Ridge a year and a half ago she'd made it clear she wanted nothing to do with him. Except when she was giving him unreasonable deadlines and reminding him of his civic duty. Yeah, well, he wasn't in the military anymore. He took orders from no one but himself.

Glancing back out the window, he couldn't help but watch Sutton watching him through a massive pair of sunglasses that covered half her face. She did not look happy. Casey frowned.

"What's wrong, Boss?" asked his newest employee. Isabella—Isadora—he couldn't remember, exactly. Understandable, considering his manager had hired the teenager and today was her first day on the job.

She was still wiping down a nearby table, wearing curiosity on her face, and clearly waiting for an answer to her question. "I didn't say anything."

"No, but you made a sound deep in your throat, kind of like a cross between a groan and a grunt."

"I do that sometimes. You'll get used to me."

"Yeah, okay." She looked about to say more.

He cut her off. "Run into the stockroom and grab more bags of coffee beans and cookie tins.

When you come back, see if you can make these displays look more appealing."

"Yeah, okay." She nodded and hurried away.

Alone again, Casey ventured another glance out the window.

Sutton was on the move, pushing through the crowd, her steps determined, her lips twisted in disapproval. He made that sound in his throat again.

As if hearing him, which was physically impossible, Sutton yanked off the sunglasses. The gesture revealed ice-blue eyes that sought, found and then hooked on him. Casey continued rearranging the table display while simultaneously pretending he hadn't seen her. Tricky, since he was currently sharing some pretty significant eye contact with the woman.

He was just about to turn away when a flash of movement caught his attention. Casey instantly dropped his gaze. A hard pang shot through his chest. Sutton wasn't alone. Of course she wasn't alone. No school today, which meant she had her seven-year-old son with her. Now Casey had to swallow back a wave of grief and sorrow.

The sensation dug deeper when Sutton leaned down and said something to the little boy.

Toby lowered his head. She continued talking. The kid continued staring at his feet. When she tugged affectionately on a lock of his dark brown hair, Toby lifted one shoulder in a move so reminiscent of his father, a different kind of grief and sorrow moved through Casey. It was like being given a glimpse into someone else's loss. Though the pain was all his.

He blamed the sting in his eyes on the overwhelming variety of scents assaulting him. Not the sight of a little boy and his mother, neither of whom belonged to him.

Turning away, he retreated to a spot behind the counter and got busy filling orders. With his hands expertly working the espresso machine, Casey tried not to notice Sutton and Toby entering the shop. He tried not to notice Sutton's determined footsteps, or the way Toby reluctantly followed after her, looking bored and miserable. Problem was, Casey's attention was always captured by the tall, willowy blonde and the little boy who looked so much like his dad.

Casey wasn't the only one watching the mayor marching toward him like a five-star general on the eve of an important battle. A table full of women not only noticed Sutton bearing down on him, but they also had a few things to say.

"…she's going to read him the riot act…"

"…serves him right for not decorating…"

"…I remember when the two of them were an item…"

"…she married that other boy, his best friend…"

Those were only a few of the snippets Casey caught. He tuned out the rest and braced for another lecture from Sutton as mayor. The one he probably—possibly—okay, definitely—deserved.

She stopped at the counter. He ignored her. Preferring, instead, to work the espresso machine with the same single-minded focus he'd once applied to the controls in the cockpit of his F-22 Raptor.

Sutton was having none of it. "Nice try, Casey. We both know you see me."

He did not sigh. Although, he may have indulged in the guy equivalent. Hard to know for certain with the steamer barreling along full speed ahead.

Undeterred by his lack of communication, or the busybodies leaning in their direction, Sutton slapped a piece of glossy paper on the counter between them.

That, too, he ignored.

She cleared her throat. Twice. Then, with a perfectly manicured fingertip, slid the Christmas flyer a few inches closer to him.

More ignoring on his part. A man could do a lot of that while steaming milk.

"I assume you have an explanation for me," she said over the din. "Perhaps a natural disaster, or grave personal illness? Maybe an emergency in the foothills of the Alaskan mountains, something along those lines?"

He so enjoyed being patronized. Although, to be fair, he had used each of the above excuses in the past week, whenever she pushed him to get busy decorating the exterior of his shop. At least one of them being true...ish.

"Well?"

Abandoning his post, Casey handed off the half-finished latte to a waiting employee and stared at Sutton. "Well, what?"

She drew in an audible breath. "Why isn't the outside of your shop decorated for Christmas? The deadline was, as you well know—" she tapped the flyer "—two days ago."

He had no defense. None she'd accept, at any rate.

Instead of answering, he turned his attention to her miniature companion, who was watching their conversation with interest. Those big round eyes and gloomy expression punched through Casey's resolve to remain neutral when it came to other people's kids. Particularly this one. Toby Wentworth got to him, every time. "Hey, little man, why the sad face?"

"My mom is making me *shop* with her." The boy heaved a dramatic sigh. "Like all day."

The kid made this announcement as if he were facing a den of angry rattlesnakes. Casey could sympathize. Back in the day, his own mom had dragged him from one store to the next in her attempt to take advantage of every Black Friday sale in town. "Fate worse than death," he said with no small amount of fervor.

"I know! What's even worse…" Toby gave his mom the side-eye "…I can't go sledding with my best friend, Samson, because I have to, you know, *shop*."

Casey knew better than to insert himself in the situation. *Not your kid. Not your place to interfere.* And yet, he did it anyway. "I have it on good authority there will be more sledding tomorrow at my sister's house." It was only one of many Evans family traditions that occurred every Thanksgiving weekend. A way to kick off the rest of the holiday season. "Quinn and her husband do it up right. There will be pizza, cake, snowman building and all kinds of kid-sized activities."

Toby gave him a smile that conveyed pure little-boy hope. "Will Samson be there?"

"You better believe it." Now that Casey's other sister, Remy, and her new husband had full custody of the boy, Samson was included in all the Evans family functions. Deciding he could endure a few hours of Christmas cheer, for Toby's sake, Casey added, "I'll be there, too, after I work the morning shift here. Consider this your official invitation."

As soon as the words left his mouth, he realized his mistake. Sutton was already scowling, her mind working frantically behind her narrowed gaze. She'd made it clear on several occasions he was never—not ever—to overstep when it came to Toby.

Casey was pretty sure inviting the boy to his sister's house fell into that category. "You're invited," he amended, holding first Toby's stare then Sutton's then Toby's again. "*If* your mother says it's okay."

The boy swung his gaze up to the woman in question. "Can I, Mom? Can I go sledding and eat pizza and stuff with Mr. Casey and Samson and the rest of their family?"

It was Sutton's turn to sigh. Casey felt her struggle and wasn't surprised when she gave the granddaddy of all noncommittal answers. "We'll see."

Toby's shoulders hunched forward. "That means no."

Casey dropped his own shoulders. It was his fault, he knew, this desire of Sutton's to avoid him and his family. It was a shame, really. She'd once been close with his sister Quinn. She'd once been close with everyone in his family, closest of all to him.

That had ended when Casey made the decision to protect a friend, at the cost of his relationship with Sutton. His heart caught at the memory and his head filled with regret.

He had a lot of regrets when it came to this woman. At one time, he'd considered her his soul mate, his confidante. His future, once they were old enough to speak wedding vows in front of a preacher.

She'd married Jeremy instead, and had given the man a son that looked just like him, all the way down to the unruly dark hair and chocolate brown eyes. "Look, Sutton, I'm sorry. I should have run this by you first. I overstepped."

"Yes, you did."

"Won't happen again."

"I'm sure it won't." She stared at him.

He stared back. Time stuttered to a standstill for a single heartbeat. Then—wonder of wonders—she slowly, tentatively, smiled at him.

He smiled back, feeling it then. The yearning. The ache. "So…" he ventured. "About tomorrow…"

She sighed, breaking their momentary connection with her reluctance.

Toby vaulted into the conversational void. "Come on, Mom. If you say yes, I promise to go shopping with you on the day after Thanksgiving every year until I'm ten."

Sutton hunkered before her son and stroked a lock of hair from his face. There was genuine affection in the move, in her eyes, in the soft smile she gave the boy. And there went that pang in Casey's chest again. "Ten, huh?"

"Maybe even eleven."

She laughed. "We'll discuss it later. In the meantime…" She rose, tossed her shoulders back, and set her body language to Annoyed Female. "I'd like for you to join us outside, Casey."

"Now?"

"It won't take long."

"If you haven't noticed…" He gestured to the lunch crowd currently filing into the shop and growing larger by the second. "I'm a little busy at the moment."

Their eyes locked and held. Blue on blue. One stubborn will against another. "Make yourself unbusy."

"No can do."

"I mean it, Casey. Outside." Her voice held all the annoyance he saw swimming in her gaze earlier. "Now."

The woman was relentless, and clearly not giving up. He knew when he was beat. To quote his newest employee, "Yeah, okay."

He swung a bar towel over his shoulder, rounded the counter and gestured for Sutton to lead the way. When she just stood there, he cocked a brow and added with mock patience, "After you, Ms. Mayor."

With a huff, she spun on her heel and paraded toward the exit, head held high.

Casey attempted to follow, but Toby tugged on his arm. "I should probably warn you. My mom was using her irritated voice just now. That means—" the boy looked left, then right "—you're in big trouble."

"Don't I know it, pal."

As she wove her way through the crowded coffee shop, Sutton kept her face free of all expression. There were too many eyes on her, on Casey and her son, on all of them. She didn't want to give their spectators more reason to gossip. Even now, she could hear people wondering what she planned to say to the man once she had him outside.

Sutton wasn't sure herself.

All she knew was that she had to convince him to decorate the exterior of his business. The future of Thunder Ridge depended on his cooperation. Okay, that was a slight exaggeration. Decorating Main Street was only the first step in winning a spot on the travel magazine's top-ten list of best Christmas towns in America. It was also the easiest. If Sutton couldn't get Casey on board with this simple task, how would she get him to agree to the rest?

She could feel him at her back. He was making

Toby laugh, a feat in and of itself. Her son was usually shy around strangers. Casey wasn't exactly a stranger, but close enough. Yet, she could hear the two bonding over her earlier attempt to put some authority in her voice.

*It means you're in big trouble.*

True, but Sutton had to play this one very carefully. She needed Casey on her side. He was Thunder Ridge royalty. As the oldest of six siblings from the town's most respected family, he had considerable pull with his fellow residents. If he participated in the Christmas activities the city council had planned, others would follow. If he pushed back, others would do the same.

Various customers shouted out greetings to him, a few slapped his back, one or two shook his hand. Sutton received her own share of hellos and "how ya doings," but none as warm as the ones directed at Casey. That was Casey. Mr. Popularity. Sutton, not so much. Even after winning the mayoral election, she was still the outsider, still the girl who never quite fit in.

She took a quick glance over her shoulder, caught Toby grinning up at the man with little-boy wonder. Sutton hadn't seen that level of awe in her son since his father died two years ago. A beat of sorrow—and a few too many what-ifs—lodged in her throat. She pushed them away with a short intake of air and exited the building. A gust of cold air slapped her in the face. The frigid wind waged a ruthless battle with the midday sun, and was clearly winning.

Speaking of winning...

With the contest on her mind, and her breath swirling in a cloud around her head, she took up a position facing Cargo Coffee. Casey settled in beside her, standing shoulder to shoulder, his impressive height and broad shoulders making her feel delicate. At nearly five feet, ten inches she rarely felt delicate. Toby squished in between them as harried shoppers rushed by. A few looked their way, but, as if sensing the tension, none stopped to chat.

"All right, Casey," Sutton said over her son's head. "Tell me what you see."

"Hmm." He placed his forefinger on his chin, then made a grand show of angling his head to the left, then the right, then the left again. "I spy with my little eye..."

Toby snickered. "Good one, Mr. Casey."

"My man." The two bumped fists.

Sutton sighed. Of course, he would turn this whole thing into a joke. She gave him a crushing look of impatience. He did not fall to his knees. "Be serious, please. Just this once."

"Yeah, yeah. If you insist..." Another grand show on his part.

Another sigh on hers.

"I see," he began, tapping his chin in thoughtful contemplation. "A well-designed, perfectly appropriate business facade that meets Thunder Ridge's current building code."

"Want to know what I see?" she asked, giving him no time to answer. "I see a glaring disregard for a simple request from your mayor. A request that, if followed, will help Thunder Ridge win a national competition that will bring in tourists from all over the country, and thereby benefit local businesses, Cargo Coffee included."

Toby blinked up at her. "Huh?"

She smiled down at her confused son and translated in a soft voice. "Simply put, sweetie, Mr. Evans didn't decorate his coffee shop like I asked him to."

"Oh, yeah. I know."

Casey opened his mouth to reply, but Toby beat him to it. "Your building does kind of stick out, Mr. Casey, and not in a good way. I mean, don't you *like* Christmas decorations?"

The question, asked so innocently, seemed to give the man pause. Sutton thought she saw something sad move into his eyes. But it was gone before she could decipher the expression. "Sure, kid," he said, the words coming out flat and unemotional. "I like them okay."

"Then how come you didn't put up any lights or ornaments or stuff?"

*Out of the mouths of babes*, Sutton thought, trying not to smile in satisfaction. Hard to do, because, really, her son was pretty amazing. The best thing she'd ever done. Her heart filled with so much love and affection that she had to swallow or find herself tearing up.

This was not the moment to turn sentimental.

"I guess time got away from me," Casey said in his defense. His tone implied there was more to the story, *much* more. But Toby was too young to recognize the underlying apathy in the words, or detect the hint of bitterness.

Sutton had no such problem and for a moment she could only blink in surprise. Christmas used to be Casey's favorite holiday. She had pictures to prove it. And memories. So many memories. What happened to turn him off the holiday?

"Casey, I…" She paused, not sure what she meant to say.

His head lifted and their gazes connected. In the ensuing silence, she noticed how his blue, blue eyes were full of secrets. Secrets that hadn't always been there. Secrets that caused him great pain. Unable to stop herself, she reached to him. "Casey…"

He shifted away from her, his blue eyes curious beneath his nearly black hair and equally dark eyebrows. "Why is winning the contest so important to you, Sutton?"

She let her hand drop and shook her head in defeat. That he had to ask told her how little he understood her now. Maybe he'd never understood her. Maybe that was why he'd betrayed her trust and broken her heart. And…this wasn't about her. *Or* him. "Thunder Ridge is a special place any time of the year, but even more so at Christmas. The town and her citizens deserve national recognition. As mayor, I'm determined to make that happen."

"Sutton Fowler, still swinging for the fences."

His words made her bristle, as he probably knew they would. After all, he knew her history better than most. Knew how hard she'd worked to prove she was more than the girl whose mother abandoned her and her alcoholic father when she was barely older than Toby was now. And yet, here he was, judging her for wanting to do the best job she could, for the betterment of the town. "I'm not Sutton Fowler anymore," she ground out. "I'm Sutton Wentworth."

Casey's face went perfectly blank. "Right. Sutton *Wentworth*." The blankness stayed for one beat, two. Then, for a millisecond, it was as if a mask peeled away from his face, and all that was left was an expression of grief and bone-deep sorrow. How well she knew the feeling.

Time to wrestle back some semblance of control. "Just decorate your building…okay?"

"Or what?"

Feeling her frustration rise all over again, she warned, "You don't want to mess with me, Casey."

Humor twisted at his lips, then moved into his eyes and, there, in that amused expression, was a glimpse of the fun-loving boy who had stolen her heart once upon a time. "Hold on." He patted around in his pockets, came up with a pen. "Let me jot that down." He opened his palm and began furiously scribbling. "Don't... Mess... With... Sutton."

Toby giggled. Casey winked at the boy.

Surprisingly, Sutton felt her own lips twitch. The snarky response was pure Casey Evans. The only person who could make her laugh when all she wanted to do was cry. She would not be swayed by the reminder. "Decorate your building," she said. "Or I'll do it myself. And I'll go as bright and as festive and as tacky as I possibly can."

"Well, then. When you put it that way," he readjusted his stance and grinned smugly. "I'll get right on it."

Something in his voice... "Are you crossing your fingers behind your back?"

"No, ma'am."

"Then let me see your hands."

Before he could obey, a teenage girl wearing a

green-and-gold Cargo Coffee apron ducked her head out of the shop. "Hey, Mr. Evans, we need you inside. Like right now."

"On my way." He smiled down at Toby, made a mess of the already messy hair, then set his hand on the boy's shoulder. "Duty calls, kid." Hand still on her son, he looked over at Sutton. "You should really consider bringing Toby to Quinn's tomorrow. It'll be fun for you both."

He was gone before she could respond. She was still watching his retreating back when Toby tugged on her arm. "Hey, Mom?"

"Hmm?"

"Mr. Casey was crossing his fingers behind his back."

She nodded. "I know, baby. I know."

# Chapter Two

Casey's day started at 3 a.m. the next morning. Not unprecedented. His airfreight company was still a startup. That meant he was the only pilot on staff. He was also the CFO and the sole mechanic and scheduled every pickup and delivery himself. Factor in his reputation for flying in any kind of weather at any time of the day or night, and he was tapped for some of the oddest jobs in the region.

Fortunately, he'd conditioned himself to function at a high level on little sleep. The skill had served him well in the military, and continued to do so three years after his honorable discharge.

This morning proved no exception. Casey was fully awake before he disconnected from the phone call that had jolted him out of a sound sleep. He agreed to retrieve several pints of rare AB negative blood from a Denver blood bank, then deliver the lifesaving cargo to a rural hospital in southern Wyoming.

A man's life hung in the balance and the clock was ticking.

He was showered and dressed in under eight minutes. Then he went into his office and booted up his computer. A few clicks later he was on an aviation website that provided aerial views of small rural airports. He printed out a copy of the one he would be flying into and then gathered up his belongings, including his three-year-old bulldog, Winston. "Come on, old boy. We have a job to do."

The animal scrambled to his feet.

Winston's female counterpart wouldn't be making the flight this morning. Clementine's latest litter of puppies weren't yet weaned. They needed their mother. The dog's pitiful whine and woeful expression told Casey she did not like this arrangement. He knelt beside the miserable canine and gave her a good scratch behind the ears. "Come on, baby, give me a smile."

The dog snorted.

"Cheer up." He cupped Clementine's face between his palms. "Your puppies are nearly weaned and heading to their new homes soon. Then it'll be the three of us again."

Her response was a long-suffering sigh.

"I know. It's a bummer you have to stay behind and miss out on all the fun. I'll make it up to you this afternoon."

He left her taking out her frustration on one of his slippers instead of the rawhide bone he'd offered up as a bribe.

Casey Evans. Dog Whisperer.

Shaking his head, he loaded Winston into his truck. The two of them made the short journey to the hangar at Thunder Ridge Regional Airport in silence. If you didn't count Winston's snoring.

After buckling the dog into the copilot's seat, Casey put his Cessna C208 Grand Caravan through its preflight check. He was methodical and thorough, despite working against the clock.

Fortunately, the weather was good, and the skies were clear. Pickup and delivery went without a hitch. It was always gratifying to play a role in saving another human life.

By six thirty, Casey began his final approach back into Thunder Ridge. Unlike his flight out, his return trip would take him directly over the heart of town. But first, he tuned to the proper frequency and radioed for clearance. The response came seconds later.

Casey reduced power and began his initial descent. Sunrise was still a half hour away, but he could easily make out the airstrip. Beyond the two parallel rows of lights, and nearly halfway up the mountain, stood the Ice Castles, or what Casey considered one of the best things about living in Thunder Ridge during the winter months. Every year his brother McCoy and a team of local artists harvested hundreds of thousands of icicles, which they then hand-placed to create sculptures, tunnels and, as the name implied, ice castles.

Kids loved the attraction.

Casey wondered if Sutton ever took Toby up the mountain. The boy would love racing through the tunnels. *Not your business.*

Checking his airspeed, then the altimeter, he banked slightly to the right. The course correction gave him a perfect view of Main Street. Which was—go figure—all lit up like a clichéd Christmas tree. Ebenezer Grinch resisted rolling his eyes.

However, on second glance, Casey could admit, albeit reluctantly, that Thunder Ridge looked pretty amazing all dressed up for the holidays. If the contest judges traveled this same route, they would receive a spectacular view of Main Street. Including that small but significant patch of dark nothingness one block north of the town square.

Feeling the first stirrings of remorse, Casey drew in a fast intake of air. He didn't need to print out an aerial map to pinpoint the source of that glaring black hole. He was looking at his coffee shop in its stunning, unremarkable glory. Cargo Coffee, as seven-year-old Toby Wentworth had

so eloquently pointed out, did *kind of stick out,
and not in a good way.*

Another wash of guilt swirled in Casey's gut.

It was one thing to make a personal statement
for his own private reasons. It was another thing
entirely to harm Thunder Ridge's chances of winning a national contest because of hurt pride and
a lingering bitterness he couldn't quite shake.

Casey would like to think he wasn't that self-
ish. Of course, he wasn't.

He would make things right. Then spend the
bulk of the holidays in the neighboring town of
Village Green, where he'd recently opened a
second location of Cargo Coffee. He was mostly
anonymous there and, didn't know the mayor per-
sonally. It was a good plan. A win-win for all
involved. He grinned over at his passenger. "I
am a genius. Now buckle up, my friend. We're
going in."

He checked the dog's seat belt himself.

Winston gave Casey his signature perma-grin.
Heart in his throat, he patted the animal on the
head. "You're a good boy. The best of the best."

The dog licked his hand, leaving a trail of bulldog slobber.

"Gross."

He was rewarded with another slobbery swipe
of the tongue. Casey shook his head. "You are a
shameless, ill-mannered savage."

"Arf, arf, arf!"

This time, Casey laughed, his heart filling with unfettered emotion despite the dog drool. It was in unguarded moments like these that he could feel it creeping in, the sense of gratitude for his matching pair of bulldogs. Winston and Clementine had gotten Casey through one of the roughest patches of his life, and the following two Christmas seasons since.

Most people who knew him would assume his complicated history with Sutton had something to do with his dislike of the holiday. They would be wrong. That dubious honor belonged to another woman from his more recent past. Casey Evans. Mr. Popularity. War hero and proud recipient of not one but two broken hearts.

Oh, yeah, he was some kind of special. Ebenezer Grinch with a large chip on his shoulder. He tried not to give that too much thought. He tried not to give anything *any* thought, and focused solely on landing his aircraft.

Out of the corner of his eye, he caught a movement from below. He swiveled his head and there it was again. Barely a half block north of the center of town. A flash of bold red against a black, unlit backdrop. "You have got to be kidding me."

As if attempting to follow the direction of his glare, Winston wiggled around in his seat and looked out the window. The dog gave a little bounce, started panting happily, then expressed his approval with a single bark.

The animal could not possibly see Sutton down there. Casey could hardly see her. It was more like he *sensed* her. Still, he pointed at the dog. "You big fat traitor."

Seemingly unimpressed with the name-calling, Winston settled back into his seat. And promptly fell asleep.

Casey continued frowning.

Sutton shouldn't be out at this hour. Yesterday's snow would have turned to ice. The streets would be slippery. The sidewalks even more so. What was the woman thinking?

Less than twenty-four hours after issuing her ultimatum, the mayor had taken matters into her own hands. Casey would let her know what he thought of her impatience. Once he got himself and his snoring bulldog safely on the ground.

He banked slightly to the left. Made a minuscule correction to the right. *Easy does it*. Nose slightly up. *Easy now*. He stayed airborne another few hundred feet, a few hundred more.

Then…touch down.

Mind on getting to Main Street, pronto, he taxied down the runway and went through the motions of securing the Cessna in its hangar at record speed. He transferred Winston from plane to truck, then climbed in behind the steering wheel and took off at a speed slightly over the limit.

Man and dog made the twelve-minute journey just under ten without a single spinout thanks to Casey's driving skills and the overnight efforts of the town's snowplows.

Only once he was pulling into a parking space outside his coffee shop did Casey let his mind think about the lecture he planned to give Sutton. He did *not* think about her blue eyes, long, shiny blond hair, winsome smile or high cheekbones.

He cut the engine and climbed out of the truck. Some of the tension went out of his shoulders. The sidewalks had been shoveled and salted and thus posed no immediate threat. He lifted his gaze and the tension returned. Times a million.

Sutton had been busy.

She was also currently missing from the immediate area, as was her seven-year-old son.

Casey wondered about that. Had she hired a babysitter for Toby? Or had she relied on a family member? Probably not the latter. Sutton wasn't close to her father or her uncle, even though both men were perfectly capable of sustaining healthy long-term relationships. Casey knew this because he was friends with Beau and Horace and had been for years.

Readjusting his stance, he took a more thorough inventory of the damage done to his building. Sutton was a woman of her word. She'd been productive since he'd landed his plane, turning on some sort of secret switch or something. She'd gone bright and festive and as tacky as possible. Casey could only shake his head.

The lights weren't so bad, if a man enjoyed a mild case of retina burn. The miles of garland were almost acceptable, as were the ornaments and little silver bells and the wire-framed trio of reindeer taking up residence near the front door. But…oh no. No, no, no. The six-foot plastic Santa under the awning was a step too far.

Without pausing, or thinking too hard about what he was doing, Casey grabbed the tacky decoration. He stuffed the monstrosity under his arm like an oversize football, turned toward his truck and came to a dead stop.

Sutton stood directly in his path. She did not look happy. In fact, she'd planted her feet shoulder width apart and jammed her hands on her hips. Her face also looked stern. It was a pose, Casey knew, to hide the fact that he'd caught her by surprise.

Good. Shifted the balance of power into his hands. Taking the unexpected gift, he decided to wait her out.

She adopted the same tactic, her silence giving him a chance to take a good look at her in the dawn's early-morning light. He pretended not to notice the way his heart pounded hard in his chest. Or the way she'd left her long, silver-blond hair hanging loose around her shoulders. Or how her festive red coat highlighted her pale coloring, or how the black jeans she wore emphasized her mile-long legs.

Nope, he didn't notice any of that.

She took her own silent appraisal of him, then bit her lower lip, a gesture from their childhood that left Casey feeling mildly unsettled. Something vaguely like homesickness stirred within him, the memory from another day, another time.

Now he was the one caught by surprise.

As if sensing the power shifting back in her direction, Sutton took charge. She pointed a finger at him. "Where do you think you're going with Santa?"

Casey didn't answer. Why state the obvious?

Clearly unmoved by the silent treatment, Sutton took a step closer. "I know you're not attempting to steal public property."

"No, ma'am," he said in his most reasonable voice. The one he used with unhappy customers and surly town mayors. "I am not stealing public property. I am *relocating* public property."

Her eyes narrowed. "Relocating where?"

"To the bed of my pickup truck."

"Put Santa back where you found him. I mean it, Casey. Put him back."

"You mean, put *it* back," he countered, splitting hairs, mostly just to be ornery. "It's a plastic Christmas decoration, Sutton, not a real person."

He heard the little catch in her voice right before she lunged. Anticipating the move, he dodged to his left. To the right. Left. Right. Sutton easily kept up the pace.

They engaged in another series of bobs and weaves, and then she sprang forward. Her outstretched hands connected with the plastic Santa. Casey yanked it away.

Too late. She'd already taken hold of the head.

Recognizing how foolish he was being, yet unable to stop himself, he yanked again. "Let go."

Sutton held on for dear life. "Not a chance."

They struggled a moment longer, each refusing to give ground and probably looking as ridiculous as Casey felt. It was as if they'd entered some weird time continuum and were back to their ten-year-old selves. What next? Name-calling and sticking out tongues?

He wasn't sure who lost their footing first. All he knew was that they were going down, hard, and if he didn't act fast, one of them was going to end up hurt, probably Sutton.

Santa forgotten, Casey rotated to his right, bent at the knees, reached out his arms and caught her around the waist seconds before she face-planted onto the sidewalk.

* * *

As a former trial attorney in one of the largest cities in the world, Sutton was no stranger to uncomfortable situations. Some were of her own making. A few had required a bit of soul-searching after the fact. However, none, not one single instance, had lowered her to the level of her current humiliation.

She only had herself to blame. She'd behaved badly.

But then, so had Casey.

Time to regain some of her lost dignity. But how? She was currently bent at the waist, caught in the man's strong, capable hands. She didn't dare wiggle. She hardly let herself breathe. One slip on Casey's part, one stumble on hers, and she'd be in a significant lip-lock with a six-foot plastic Santa.

What. A. Catastrophe.

"Well, well, well," said the man standing between her and certain disaster. "Looks like we have ourselves a predicament."

Talk about overstating the obvious.

Sutton shut her eyes. "Help me up, Evans. I mean it. Help me up. Now."

The demand earned her a chuckle. "Ask nicely."

She tried not to grit her teeth. "Please."

"Please, what?"

His ongoing amusement only managed to increase her irritation. He suffered no remorse at all. He thought the situation was *funny*. This time, she did grit her teeth. "*Please*, help me up."

"Was that so hard?"

Brutal. "Casey, I'm warning you—"

"Yeah, yeah, yeah. Help you up or else." With one masterful swoop, he hauled her upright. She dangled in the air for a second, eyes locked with his, and then her toes met the snow-dusted pavement, followed by her heels.

"Thanks."

"No problem."

They both just stood there, unmoving, staring. Staring. It took her a moment to realize Casey's hands were still on her waist. "You can let go now."

He did. Abruptly. Too abruptly. She immediately lost her balance. Arms waving frantically, she nearly righted herself, then overcorrected. Perfect. She was going down again. Going down hard.

She braced for impact.

But then, that same set of big capable hands gripped her shoulders. "Whoa there, Sutton. Easy now. I got you."

*I got you.* Oh boy, did he ever. She felt the heat from his palms seeping through her coat, offering support, comfort. Everything he'd once given her without a second thought. She tried not to let her mind travel back in time to happier days, or to notice how Casey stood perfectly still, his eyes searching her face. "You okay?" he asked.

Sure, *now* he acted like a gentleman. Where were the witty comments? The insulting reminders that she'd brought this on herself? "I'm good," she lied, shrugging out from beneath his hands. "Really, I'm okay."

She was so not okay.

She was ashamed, embarrassed and generally mortified by her juvenile behavior. What had possessed her to engage in such a ridiculous tug-of-war? Over a plastic Santa Claus, no less?

Sutton was usually a sensible person. The sensible thing to do would be to take what self-esteem she had left and leave. So why couldn't she get her feet moving? Why couldn't she look away from Casey's concerned expression? The one she hadn't seen since their last night as a couple over a decade ago.

"You sure you're all right?" he asked again. "You seem, kind of, I don't know…shaky."

Mr. Popularity was now Mr. Perceptive?

"I'm good, Casey." Except, she wasn't. Still dizzy from being held upside down, she struggled to keep from swaying.

By contrast, Casey was perfectly steady, looking far too appealing with his jaw darkly stubbled and in need of a shave. Not to mention the brown leather bomber jacket that suggested he was born to be bad. The man was supposed to have grown a paunch and lost all his hair. But, oh no. Casey Evans had only gotten better with age.

Her heart took a sudden nosedive. Stupid heart.

"Not to belabor the point—" he gave her a fast head-to-toe once-over "—but I'm having a hard time buying your 'I'm okay' nonsense."

Nonsense? "That's because you have a suspicious mind."

It was the wrong thing to say. His expression instantly closed. Gone was the warm humor, the soft eyes, the easygoing manner. "No, Sutton, that would be you."

"For good reason," she snapped. Who was this contentious woman inhabiting her body? Her normal self was professional and pleasant. But there were things about Casey that played on her nerves. Her very last nerve.

Take for instance, now.

He was standing too close, close enough that she had to tilt her head up to see his face. She felt a spasm of something sharp and forlorn in her heart, bleaker than loneliness, but not quite qualifying as grief. And certainly not guilt. Casey had been the one to ruin things between them, not Sutton. He'd brought alcohol to her eighteenth birthday party. Even knowing the toll her father's substance abuse had taken on her family, on *her*, he'd supplied beer to their friends.

When the cops arrived, Casey had taken full responsibility. Most seventeen-year-old boys would have made excuses, or they would have flat-out lied. Not Casey. He'd accepted the blame without hesitation, which had given Sutton hope they could work through the incident. But the next day, when she'd begged him for answers, he'd remained stubbornly silent. In her eyes, his refusal to explain his behavior had been his real offense, the one that had torn them apart.

As though sensing the direction of her thoughts and wishing to be anywhere but here with her, drumming up ancient history, he sighed heavily.

Her sentiments exactly.

"Look, Sutton, I'm sorry I didn't get around to decorating my shop."

She started to speak.

He cut her off with a hand in the air. "In my defense, you didn't give me much of a chance. We only spoke about it yesterday."

*Oh, how quickly they forget.* "Not true. I brought it up on several occasions. You had an entire month to get it done. Yesterday was my third and final ultimatum, one you clearly didn't take seriously."

"I took it seriously." He sounded affronted.

It was an act. She'd cross-examined enough

witnesses to recognize a false testimony when she heard one. She called his bluff. "You had your fingers crossed behind your back."

His laugh was either amused or contrite. Hard to tell.

Sutton didn't have time for this. Neither of them did. "Well, the decorating is complete. Or nearly so, once I put up a few more lights in your doorway and return Santa to his prime position under the awning."

She bent to pick up the decoration.

Casey moved a split second faster. With a single motion, he liberated the oversize ornament from its ignoble position. Sutton thought about making another grab for Santa, but that would be childish. She used her words instead. "Casey, you're being unnecessarily stubborn. It's just a Christmas decoration. It's not—"

"No, Sutton. Just…no. I'll accept the rest." He nodded toward the building. "Even the twinkling reindeer. But I will not tolerate a tacky six-foot Santa Claus."

"He isn't tacky."

"Oh, yes, he is."

She opened her mouth to argue, but couldn't quite push the words past her lips. The Santa *was* tacky. There had been any number of tasteful options. But she'd included the horrible monstrosity out of spite, which was not very Christian of her.

She should ask for forgiveness. And she would, tomorrow. At church. Right now, she had to concentrate on the battle at hand.

"Take the loss, Sutton."

It wasn't in her nature. Even as kids, when Casey pulled one of his infamous practical jokes, she would do whatever it took to one-up him.

"You know I'm right about this," he said, readjusting his hold on Santa. "Although, I'll give you points for creativity." He did it then. He crossed the proverbial line and pulled out his boyish grin. The lopsided version that included a slight head tilt.

She blinked. That smile, it made her momentarily forget what they were arguing about.

Taking advantage of her hesitation, he sidestepped her and headed straight for his truck.

Sutton watched, oddly mesmerized, as his long legs churned up the short distance with ease. Casey was a big guy, professional-football-player big, but he had a way of moving through the world with the speed and agility of a sprinter.

Out in the street, he glanced over his shoulder, winked at her, then dumped Santa unceremoniously in the flatbed. "Now that that's settled—" he ambled across the small divide between them "—let's talk about the fun and games at my sister's house. Are you accepting my invitation or not?"

"Why do you ask?"

"You know why."

Sadly, she did. If she said yes, he would want to warn his sister she was coming. Quinn would not be happy. She still held it against Sutton for not standing by Casey after the party. Well, Sutton wasn't all that thrilled to hang out with her former friend, either.

Toby, however, would be beyond excited. He'd been unable to talk about anything else since Casey issued the invitation.

Sutton tried to think only of her son. She really did. But Casey had just made this personal. *Very* personal. Under the circumstances, there was only one way to respond. "Tell Quinn to expect us sometime around noon."

# Chapter Three

With her son at his grandfather's house, Sutton spent the rest of the morning in her office procrastinating on tasks that could have waited until Monday. Better to focus on work than allow her mind to wander back to Casey. To remember the feel of his hands on her shoulders or the way his eyes had wavered between humor and concern. Then...disappointment.

So much for putting the man out of her mind.

Ever since their recent encounters, all she could think about was their past, which only enhanced her guilt and sense of betrayal. Jeremy had been a part of her childhood, too, nearly as important to her as Casey. Good, Better, Best, that was what they'd named themselves. Sutton couldn't remember why they'd chosen to take on the moniker, or which of them was which, but the label had stuck through childhood and into their teen years, only dropped after the night of her birthday party and the fallout afterward.

Loyal to them both, Jeremy hadn't taken sides after the big breakup. He'd also been the one to keep in touch with Sutton after high school. Emails, phone calls, personal visits. Always there, always supportive, always a trustworthy friend, until their relationship had become something more. They'd had a good life together, not perfect, but good.

Sutton had no regrets.

Sighing, she reached for the photograph she kept on her desk. She'd taken the shot herself, catching Jeremy in a candid moment. He'd been manning the grill and had glanced at her over his shoulder, a ready smile on his face. Her eyes filled with tears at the happy memory. She touched the image, sighing again. It was like looking at her son in twenty years.

Jeremy had been an attentive husband and father. When he was home. Which hadn't been often, due to his job as a combat helicopter pilot. Sutton had never begrudged his dedication to the military, not even when the two solemn-faced airmen had shown up on her doorstep to shatter her life with the news of her husband's death.

That had been two years ago. She was better now, stronger, certainly less sad. She'd made the right decision to come back to Thunder Ridge.

Toby deserved a childhood in the same small town where his parents had grown up. Where neighbors helped neighbors and holidays were celebrated with enthusiasm and joy.

Sutton couldn't imagine raising her son anywhere else. And now, finally, her priorities were back in place. She mowed through a pile of contracts that needed her signature. Then read up on Thunder Ridge's fire codes in anticipation of the tree-lighting ceremony next week.

She was still wading through the technical language when her cell phone dinged with an incoming text. Half-distracted, she scrolled open the screen and read the short message. Only two words. You're welcome. The sender had also provided a picture of…was that her house? She peered closer.

"He didn't. He wouldn't." Just to be sure, she enlarged a section of the grainy image. Her lips twitched. No, she would not laugh. The man had gotten her back, all right. But…how? *How did he pull that off*?

One way to find out.

She stabbed the call button with her fingertip.

Casey answered on the second ring. "I'm very busy and important, Sutton. Please state your business in quick, concise language."

She would not laugh. She counted to five instead. "What is that hideous Santa doing on the roof of my house?"

"Just part of my relocation plan. You're welcome."

"Very funny, Casey. Take him down, ASAP. I want him off my—"

She was talking to dead air.

Torn between calling him back and coming up with ways to get even, she sat back in her chair and thought through her options. Several came to mind, all involving a tacky Santa, none she could do on her own. She had an entire staff at her disposal. But no, that would be a gross misuse of taxpayer money.

Her concentration blown, she called it quits for the day and made the short trip to her father's house. She didn't have far to go, barely three blocks from her office.

She parked on the street and, after climbing out of her car, studied her childhood home nestled in a row of similarly built one-story structures. When Sutton was a child, the cluster of houses had made up a sort of makeshift artists' colony.

With considerable money from a developer, the tiny homes were now quirky yet exclusive rentals. All except one. Her father had been the lone holdout, refusing to sell. The anemic string of lights and small wreath on the door meant more work for her. When would she find the time? A problem for another day.

At least her father took decent care of the property now that he was clean and sober. Sutton tried to think of him as the man he was today, not as the one he'd been during her formative years. But she couldn't stop her mind from drumming up the past.

Beau Fowler hadn't been a mean drunk. He hadn't been abusive or any of the usual clichés portrayed in movies and books. He'd simply hated being alone. And so he'd surrounded himself with people, in his own home, nearly every night of the week, the alcohol flowing freely.

To this day, Sutton hated large gatherings. It wasn't the crowds. It was the laughter and raised voices. The sounds transported her back to her childhood. When she'd lain awake in bed, a pillow over her head, praying desperately for the noise to stop so she could fall asleep.

*It's in the past.*

She'd forgiven her father. The Lord had provided healing for them both. And yet, there was a distance between them that neither knew how to breach. That wasn't the case with Toby. Her son adored his grandfather. And Beau Fowler was proving to be a good role model.

Grateful for that, Sutton approached the front door and paused, instantly shaken by the sound of blaring Christmas music. And the hearty laughter. She was being ridiculous, she knew. She shrugged off the spurt of melancholy and reached for the doorknob.

After a twist and a small shove, she was inside the entryway. "Hello? Anybody home?"

No answer.

Following the voices muffled beneath Bing Crosby's masterful crooning, she stepped into the tiny kitchen. Her heart swelled at the sight of Toby and her father bent over a half-completed puzzle, faces screwed up in two identical scowls of concentration. She'd always thought Toby inherited his looks from Jeremy. Now she also saw her own father reflected in the boy.

For a moment, she simply watched the two at play, taking note of her son first, then the man who'd raised her. He looked better than he had in years. Tall like her, he was skinny as a zipper with a head full of silver hair. Add in the bushy eyebrows, the equally bushy beard, maybe put him in a red suit and he'd resemble an underfed Santa.

Clearly, she had Santa on the brain.

She wasn't the only one.

"I'm telling you, kiddo," her father said to Toby. "When it comes to delivering presents, Santa knows his stuff."

"But Grandpa," the boy argued while simultaneously rummaging through a pile of puzzle pieces, "how's he supposed to get inside our house? We don't have a chimney."

"Santa will find a way. He always does."

"I don't know…" Toby snapped a piece in place, then dug around for another. "Should I, maybe, leave a window open, or something?"

"Well, hmm…" Her father pretended to ponder the possibility. "That's not a bad idea."

Sutton gaped. It was a terrible idea. They lived in the mountains. The temperatures dipped below freezing nearly every night at this time of year.

"Then again," her father said before Sutton could interject a few facts about frostbite, "I think you should trust Santa to get the job done on his own."

Sutton had heard enough. She cleared her throat.

Two heads turned in her direction.

An instant later, Toby was bulleting across the floor. "Mom! You're finally here." The boy skidded to a stop mere inches short of slamming into her. "Is it time to go to Miss Quinn's?"

"Whenever you're ready."

"I'm ready. I'm ready right now. Come on, let's go." He took off for the door.

Sutton caught him two steps later. Dragging him back around to face her, she looked meaningfully at his feet. "Maybe let's put on your snow boots first."

Toby glanced down at his socks and let out a belly laugh. "Oh, yeah. That'd probably be smart."

"Even smarter if we add your coat, scarf and ski cap."

Still laughing, the little boy sped back to the table—the child was always in a hurry—then dropped to his hands and knees.

While her son searched for the discarded footwear, Sutton took the opportunity to address her father. "Hi, Dad."

He nodded a greeting, saying nothing, his eyes guarded and carefully blank. His gaze looked, she suspected, very similar to her own.

Sighing, she adopted what she hoped was a neutral tone. "Thanks for watching Toby this morning. I owe you one."

"You owe me nothing, Sutton. I like spending time with my grandson. He's a good kid. What do you say, Toby?" He reached down and ruffled the boy's hair. "We'll finish the puzzle next time you stop by."

"That would be great." Toby plopped his bottom on the ground, stuffed his feet inside the now-rescued boots, then bounced back up. "Thanks for hanging out with me today."

"Anytime, son. Anytime. Now give me a hug and go have fun with your friends."

Toby launched himself into the man's open arms. "See you later, Grandpa."

"Count on it." Still hugging the boy, her father said, "Take pictures, will you?"

"Of course."

Another awkward moment passed. Then Toby was grabbing his coat and racing for the door and Sutton was chasing after him, shouting over her shoulder, "Bye, Dad."

On the drive across town, Toby kept up a running commentary about puzzles, puppies and the proper way to sled down a hill. Then came the rapid-fire questions. "Do you think Miss Quinn made chocolate cupcakes? If so, can I have two? I wonder if Mr. Casey is already there? Do you think he brought puppies with him?"

Sutton waited for her son to draw a breath. "I'm sure she made chocolate cupcakes." Quinn owned a business that specialized in all things chocolate. Cupcakes were always on the menu at her house. "You can have one. We'll discuss a second, depending on what else you eat."

"I guess that's fair."

"As to your other questions, Mr. Casey is probably already there, or will be soon. Will he bring puppies? We'll have to wait and see."

She spent the rest of the ride fielding questions and praying Casey had left his adorable baby bulldogs at home. One look at the little guys and she'd fall in love with each and every one of them. Sutton didn't have time for a puppy. Nor did she want to engage in yet another discussion with her son about all the reasons why. The talk never ended well.

"I don't see Mr. Casey's truck," Toby said the moment she turned into Quinn's drive. "I guess he's not here yet."

"I guess not." Sutton didn't see Casey's truck or his '63 Mustang or the GTO, aka the Goat. The man had a passion for restoring vintage automobiles. He also had a thing for skiing black diamond runs, skydiving into the valley and sailboarding across Thunder Ridge Lake.

All of which Sutton enjoyed, as well, though she hadn't indulged for years. It pained her to admit privately how much she and Casey had in common. Pulling her car to a stop behind a red Jeep, she cut the engine. "Ready to go inside?" she asked her son.

"Ready!"

They exited the car at the same time. Sutton from behind the steering wheel, purse straps thrown over her shoulder. Toby from the back seat, a literal bounce in his step.

As they made their way to the front door, Sutton took in Quinn's house with the eyes of a town mayor hoping to win a national Christmas contest. She liked what she saw. The rambling two-story home was nestled on the banks of Thunder Ridge Lake and had the quintessential wraparound porch. Quinn had decorated the exterior tastefully and with a heavy hand that did Sutton's heart proud.

Thousands of white twinkling lights—*not* an exaggeration—hung from every roofline and easement. Golden wire reindeer with red bows around their necks fed on a blanket of snow. Shrubs sparkled, trees dazzled, and not a single plastic Santa in sight. "I like how Miss Quinn decorated her house," Toby said, eyes wide.

"Me, too," Sutton admitted. No wonder the woman was the five-time champion of the Thunder Ridge Christmas Lights Neighborhood Challenge.

"I wonder if the inside is as nice as the outside."

As if on cue, the front door swung open. Quinn herself exited the house, looking perfectly put together and comfortable in her own skin. Sutton had always liked that about her former friend. She'd liked a lot of things about Quinn Evans, or rather Quinn Holloway now that she'd married Grant. Despite the name change, there was no denying the woman had been born an Evans. She had the same black hair and blue, blue eyes as the rest of her siblings.

The Evans clan shared some strong DNA. They also had a fondness for dogs, loved each other without question, and were loyal to a fault. They welcomed anyone and everyone into their fold. However, they also had long memories. When you crossed one Evans, you crossed them all.

"Hi, Quinn."

"Hello." She spared Sutton only the briefest of glances, quick and impersonal, before addressing her son with a full, welcoming smile. "Hey, Toby."

"Hey, Miss Quinn. Is Samson here yet?"

"He's in the kitchen with the other kids, taking advantage of the hot chocolate buffet."

The little boy beamed. "You made hot chocolate?"

Quinn laughed. "You bet I did. I also provided marshmallows, whipped cream, candy canes and sprinkles. But don't take my word for it, go on inside and see for yourself."

"Can I, Mom?"

Sutton nodded. "Of course."

"All right." Toby charged up the stairs, leaving the two women facing each other in strained silence. Nothing new there.

They'd barely spoken more than a few polite sentences since Sutton had returned home, and nearly all of them pertaining to the various Christmas events scheduled in the coming weeks. Like her brother, Quinn had a lot of pull with the residents of Thunder Ridge. She was well respected and well liked, and Sutton missed having her as a friend. Quinn didn't seem to share the feeling, not if her carefully blank expression was anything to go by.

Again, Sutton broke the silence between them first. "I hope you don't mind that Casey invited Toby and me to spend the afternoon with your family."

"Toby is always welcome in my home." Sutton could practically hear her add, *You, however, are not.* But Quinn surprised her by saying, "You're also welcome, Sutton."

The woman looked ready to say more, but a crash sounded from the interior of the house. "I better see to that." Quinn turned to go, then paused at the threshold. "You coming?"

Nodding, Sutton started forward, but froze at the sound of laughter and loud music. "I… I. That is—" she swallowed "—I need a minute."

Something kind moved in Quinn's eyes, a look that told Sutton she understood her hesitation. Smiling gently, she reached out and clutched Sutton's hand. "Take your time."

Those three words, spoken in that soft manner, were enough to remind Sutton how much she'd lost the night of her eighteenth birthday. More than a boyfriend. So much more. Her heart pounded. Words stuck in her throat. It was a great relief that Quinn didn't press the issue. She simply released Sutton's hand and went inside the house.

\* \* \*

Casey saw Sutton the moment he exited his truck. She was sitting alone on his sister's porch swing bundled up against the chill in the air, eyes closed, hands in her lap. She looked lonely and lost, and that just slayed him. Sutton had hurt him, no getting around that. But Casey had hurt her, too.

He'd never really let himself think about that part of their past. He'd been too busy taking the moral high ground. In hindsight, and at thirty-four years old, he understood his own role in their breakup. In his defense, he'd been young and confused and had thought Sutton knew him. *Surely*, she would realize there was more to the story than the one he and Jeremy told the cops.

But she hadn't trusted him. And Casey had been unable to tell her the truth. More than a misunderstanding, he'd made a promise and would take the secret to his grave. So here they were, years later, still at odds, clashing over small, insignificant offenses instead of confronting the past and putting it behind them once and for all.

Enough, Casey. *Enough*.

He bounded up the steps and stood facing Sutton, waiting for some sign that she knew he was there. She didn't move. Didn't speak. She did, however, open her eyes. Her expression wasn't especially friendly. He doubted his was, either.

They stared at one another in a kind of muted contest of wills. She blinked first. Then pushed out a soft rush of air and scooted over to make room for him on the swing. He accepted the silent invitation and sat.

Several seconds passed. Casey used the time to study Sutton's rigid profile. She was trying very hard to maintain some semblance of control, but tension rolled off her in great, giant waves. She was upset, that much he knew. What he didn't know was why.

Various reasons scudded across his mind. Had his sister said something unkind to Sutton? Had someone else in his family been confrontational? He would like to think not. His siblings were fiercely loyal, but they weren't cruel. So, what had upset her? He'd barely asked the question in his mind when he heard the overloud laughter emanating from the house, and he immediately knew the source of her discomfort.

Casey's chest tightened. He took her hand and squeezed gently.

Sighing, she turned her head and gave him a small smile. Sensation didn't just bloom in his chest, it burst, creating a mushroom cloud of unwanted emotion.

Past folded over present and it was like old times, when they didn't need to speak to know what the other was thinking. Casey didn't like it, not one bit. He pulled his hand away and considered what to say to break the silence. With Sutton, humor was always an effective tool to combat her sadness.

"Come here often?"

She gave a short bark of laughter. "Really, Casey, a lame pickup line?"

"Not lame. Smooth and sophisticated. And clearly working." He leaned toward her. "Admit it. You're into me."

She rolled her eyes. "Not even a little."

He sat back, gave his wrist a quick, nonchalant flick. "Don't blame yourself. I'm irresistible."

Another eye roll. But the left corner of her mouth quirked up. *Progress.* "Stop it, Sutton. All this gushing. You're embarrassing yourself."

Her lips twitched at both corners now. "Catch me if I swoon."

"Actually… I'd prefer a faint over a measly swoon."

"Good thing you're a man who takes disappointment well." Her voice held the stern tone of a put-upon kindergarten teacher, but her gaze had a teasing glint, and she was fighting back a smile. Casey knew the look well. Any minute she'd break into laughter.

But this was Sutton. A woman who zigged when others zagged. "Casey, seriously, don't you have something better to do than hound me?"

"Probably. But I'm not leaving until I know you're all right."

She bent her head and rubbed the spot between her eyes. "I'm fine."

Except, she wasn't.

He touched her shoulder. She flinched and he dropped his hand. "You know you don't have to go inside, Sutton. You can—"

He was cut off by the sound of the front door swinging open. Toby came rushing out of the house, his words tumbling over one another. Casey could barely keep up, but he was pretty sure he heard the words *ice castles*, *puppies*, and...wait. What? Did the kid just say *Soap Box Derby*?

Casey's mouth went dry and his heart rattled in his chest like some kind of wild animal stuck in a trap.

Clearly more competent at deciphering her son's garbled speech, Sutton held up her hand to stop the boy's rambling. "Yes, of course I knew about the Soap Box Derby. It was my idea to re-instate the race. Not only will it be fun, it'll also impress the magazine judges."

A spurt of astonishment wound through him. This was Sutton's doing? He wasn't sure why that surprised him. As mayor, it was well within her purview to resurrect a popular event that had once been a Christmas staple in Thunder Ridge. "The cars have to be made from an approved kit, with the entrant doing most of the work under adult supervision," she told her son. "The exterior must convey the Christmas season. The winner of each division will get a big fat trophy."

Casey heard Sutton explaining the rest of the rules to her son, but only a part of his brain hooked on the words. The rest was too busy careening back in time. To the year he and Jeremy entered their first derby. They'd been about the same age as Toby was now.

Jeremy had won that race. Casey had taken the trophy the next year. By sixteen, they'd graduated from soapbox cars to the real thing, pooling together their lifesavings to buy the GTO. They'd spent every possible free moment restoring the Goat to her original glory. Sutton had been with them every step of the way, watching, sometimes joining in with Casey's hand guiding hers over the tools.

"Why didn't you tell me about the derby?" he asked in a low voice.

She stared at him. "It was highlighted on the flyer I gave you."

The flyer. Of course. The piece of paper listing all the upcoming Christmas events. He'd tossed that in the garbage after only a cursory glance. "You should have told me, anyway."

"You're right," she said, nodding slowly, looking apologetic. "I should have. I'm sorry, Casey. I thought, maybe, I—"

"Mom. Mom. *Mom!*" Toby all but shouted her name. "Did you hear me?"

She sighed. "I heard you. You said your friend Samson is entering the derby."

"His Uncle Wyatt is going to help him build the car. So can I enter, too?"

"I'm sorry, Toby. Not this year."

"How come?"

Again, her expression turned apologetic, remorseful even, as if she was only just realizing the ramifications of what resurrecting the derby would mean in her own home. "With only three weeks until the race, I'm too busy with my duties as mayor to help you build the car."

"Oh." The boy looked down at his feet. The poor kid was clearly miserable. But then, his head shot up. "That's okay. I can ask Grandpa."

Sutton's eyes widened. Casey felt his do the same. Beau Fowler was good at many things, most of them artistic in nature, but the man knew nothing about building cars. Casey, on the other hand, knew just about everything there was to know. But it would mean overstepping.

Something he really, really shouldn't do.

He eyed Toby. Saw only Jeremy. If his friend were alive, Casey wouldn't be sitting here contemplating how to insert himself into the situation. Best to stay out of it. And yet, the next thing he knew, he was opening his mouth to say, "I'll help you, Toby."

"You know how to build a soapbox car, Mr. Casey?"

At the same moment he said, "As a matter of fact, I do," Sutton was saying, "I don't think that's a good idea."

"Why not?" Casey and Toby asked in unison.

"Because...." she said, looking directly at her son. "Mr. Casey is even busier than I am."

True. But a little boy needed him. Not just any little boy. Jeremy's son. "I'll make it work."

Sutton blinked. Casey could easily guess what was going on in her mind. She was making a laundry list of reasons why he wasn't the man for the job. However, once again, she surprised him. "You're sure you have time, Casey? You're absolutely certain you can build a soapbox car in three weeks?"

"A hundred percent." Better yet, it would give him a perfect excuse to avoid all the other festivities in town.

Sutton smiled at her son, who was currently vibrating with excitement. "Okay, yes, you can enter the derby with Mr. Casey's help."

Toby's hoot of delight drowned out Casey's

slightly milder cheer. "I can't wait to get started, Mr. Casey. Can Grandpa help, too?"

"Absolutely." As an artist and graphic designer, Beau would have some thoughts on how to make the exterior of the car reflect the Christmas theme.

"This is going to be so much fun."

"You know it." Casey bumped fists with the kid.

"Hey, Mom. Can I go tell Samson?"

Sutton let out a breath of amusement. "Absolutely."

Toby ran back into the house.

Casey laughed. "Now, that is one happy kid."

"Very happy. It's nice to see." A change came over Sutton, her color deepening, the small muscles around her mouth contorting with emotion. Casey understood. Toby was a great kid. The kind any parent would be proud to call son.

Suddenly uncomfortable, and needing a moment, he glanced around the porch, looking for an escape route. Before he could make his move, Sutton touched his sleeve. "Thanks, Casey."

And that was the opening he'd been looking for. "No problem. We can discuss the details inside." He stood and offered his hand. "Let's go."

She let him draw her to her feet.

They stood inches apart, momentarily frozen. Something flickered in her gaze, and Casey wondered. Guilt? Regret? No, those were the emotions swimming through him. Only then did he realize the enormous flaw in his thinking.

Spending time with Sutton's son meant spending time with Sutton.

# Chapter Four

Before Casey entered his sister's house, Sutton stopped him with a hand on his sleeve. "Hold up a sec. I have something I want to say."

He gave her a long look. Hard to read. Part considering. Mostly bored. But as he shifted to face her fully, the air between them crackled. "What's up, Sutton?"

She opened her mouth. Shut it again, sighed as the breath caught in her throat. She desperately wanted to stay in the moment, but the past tugged at her, reminding her how much she'd once cared for this man, and he for her. They'd shared their innermost secrets. Their hopes. Their dreams of a future together. They'd been of one mind, one heart. Until they weren't.

This, she realized, this urge to find a way back to him was why she kept her distance. Their time had come and gone. Why couldn't she remember that?

"Sutton…?"

She swallowed hard. "I just wanted to say thank-you, again." She carefully removed her hand from his arm. "You didn't have to offer to help Toby. I would have figured something out. Somehow, I would have—"

"I know, Sutton. You always figure something out. It's what you do." The words sounded more like a criticism than a compliment.

She tried not to flinch. "Still," she persisted, "I'm grateful and I owe you."

They were nearly the same words she'd said to her father barely an hour ago. By the look on Casey's face, they didn't sit any better with him than they had with Beau Fowler.

In fact, Casey just stood there, his face going blank. "You don't owe me anything, Sutton. Got it?" He leaned in a little closer, held her stare a beat too long. "Not one single solitary thing."

She'd insulted him. She heard it in his voice. Saw it in the way his shoulders tensed up. "I didn't mean to imply—"

"Sure you did. Although, I'm not surprised." He set his jaw and pulled back from her. "You aren't exactly gifted at accepting help from others."

Now *he'd* insulted *her.* "Look, Casey. If you want to back out, do it now, while I have time to find someone else—"

He let out a stab of laughter. "Oh no. Uh-uh. Don't throw your doubts back on me."

"I wasn't. I was simply saying there's still time to change your mind."

"Let's get a few things straight, shall we? First, I never offer to do anything I don't want to do. Second, I made a promise to a little boy and I never back out on a promise. Not. Ever. My word is solid. Golden. Unaffected by time, distance or a change in circumstances."

Sutton sensed they weren't talking about Toby or the Soap Box Derby anymore. Casey's tone was too fierce, his expression too intense, his words too pointed. She thought about asking him to clarify, but he was still talking.

"And finally, I like Toby. He's a great kid. I also like building cars. I'm good at it. Your son and I are going to have a lot of fun. It's really that simple, Sutton. Don't make this more complicated than it needs to be."

He was right. About all of it. She was over-thinking the situation. A character trait that had served her well as an attorney. But in this instance, she'd gone too far and now she felt ridiculous and defensive. Should she apologize? Maybe lighten the mood?

Definitely the latter. "Well, I guess you told me."

"I guess I did." He cracked a smile, the boyish

one that included the infamous head tilt, and just like that the tension between them was replaced by something far more potent. "So?" he asked, eyebrows lifted. "Are we heading inside now?"

"We are."

He opened the door. She followed him into a gorgeous foyer, unable to keep the awe off her face. Quinn had decorated the interior of her home with the same heavy hand she'd applied to the exterior. Crimson and gold were the dominant colors here. The garland adorning the arched doorways added a splash of green. Mistletoe hung from the one leading into a long hallway. Casey took that route, giving the bright, cheery sprig a wide berth.

Not that Sutton cared, but…okay, she cared. And, well…ouch.

Ignoring the pang of hurt, she breathed in the scent of pine and fresh-baked cupcakes. The smells reminded her of the Christmases she'd spent in the Evanses' home, first as Quinn's friend, then as Casey's girlfriend. Their mother had been kind to her. She'd taught Sutton how to cook. If not for those lessons, she and her father would have subsisted on fast food and frozen meals.

The sound of laughter and raised voices came from somewhere deep within the house. The noise level hit a crescendo and Sutton came to a dead stop, unable to move forward. Frustrated with herself, she took a deep breath. What was wrong with her? She attended work-related events all the time. Events that involved equally loud voices and laughter.

In quiet understanding, Casey waited for her to gather herself. Patience personified. She felt ridiculous and defensive all over again and barely dared to meet his eye.

"Hey, none of that, Sutton. Hey, look at me."

She did, reluctantly, and now she couldn't get enough air in her lungs.

"This isn't a party like the kind your father used to throw." He spoke in a soothing tone that matched the sympathetic look in his eyes. "We're just a bunch of family and friends and kids drinking hot chocolate, playing games, and consuming too much sugar. Good, clean fun."

It was exactly what she needed to hear. "Right, thanks. Helpful." She forced a smile.

He studied her face a moment, then grinned. "Do try to contain your enthusiasm." He slapped a hand to his heart. "My nerves can't take all this excitement."

"Hilarious."

"I know, right?" He wiggled his eyebrows. "I'm here all week."

Sutton tried not to laugh. "I'm sure someone cares. Maybe one day I will, too."

"Touching sentiment. Really. Very moving. A tear came to my eye." He mimed wiping his perfectly sculpted, very dry cheek.

She did laugh then. "To steal words from a big, dorky guy I know… I'm here all week."

"Big *and* dorky? Wow, you are terrible for my ego."

Said the man who'd given the mistletoe a wide berth only seconds before. "Same goes, Dude. Same goes."

"We find common ground at last."

"Yay, us."

Laughing, he took her hand and led her toward the back of the house. The walls were lined with an assortment of family pictures, some from the past, others taken more recently. Sutton recognized all the faces grinning back at her. Several of the shots resurrected happy memories. She let them come, let them ease her nerves.

They passed several Christmas trees along the way. Most had the red-and-gold theme she'd found in the foyer. But the tree that really caught her attention was smaller and decorated in bright, bold colors. A kids' tree. Why hadn't she thought to do that for Toby?

It wasn't too late. A trip to the big-box store on the edge of town would solve the problem. She was mentally making her shopping list when a door creaked on its hinges. The sound of shuffling feet followed. Then came a loud, earsplitting bang. She jumped. But then the noise level dropped to a low hum, indicating a mass exodus to the great outdoors had just occurred.

Sutton's suspicions were confirmed when she entered the kitchen behind Casey and discovered only a handful of adults and one large Saint Bernard gathered around the center island.

One of Casey's sisters let out a loud gasp. "Look who it is. Ebenezer Grinch himself, deigning to grace our family with his presence on this fine November day."

"Look who it is," he said without missing a beat. "My annoying little sister, Remy Evans Holcomb, running off at the mouth when nobody asked for her opinion."

So began the trading of insults. While the two bantered, Sutton took in the rest of the faces, all familiar. Wyatt Holcomb, Remy's husband and Thunder Ridge's sheriff, held a squirming baby dressed in blue-on-blue-on-blue. He was also engaged in some sort of heated discussion with Casey's brother McCoy.

Abandoning his own conversation, Casey moved in between the two men. He looked from one to the other, gave a short nod, then grabbed his brother by the arm and dragged him toward the backdoor. The giant Saint Bernard trailed behind them like a piece of gum stuck to McCoy's shoe. Right before the three crossed the threshold, Casey muttered, "Give it a rest, will ya, McCoy? If Wyatt says he'll be there, he'll be there."

Sutton wasn't sure where "there" was or what had precipitated McCoy's suspicions, but the two men were out the door before she could ask. That left Sutton with the scowling Wyatt and both of Casey's sisters. Quinn had strapped on a forward-facing child carrier, which came complete with a wide-eyed baby boy happily kicking and gurgling and grabbing for the binky his mother offered.

Remy held her own squirming bundle of joy dressed in pink-on-pink-on-pink. "Sutton," she said, smiling. "Come say hello to my adorable babies. This is Olivia. And my frowning husband is holding her twin brother, Liam."

Sutton peered at the baby girl first, then the little boy. Olivia had black hair like her mother, while Liam had inherited his father's rich auburn color. "They're gorgeous."

Remy beamed, then pressed a kiss to her daughter's forehead. "Aren't they, though?"

Still frowning, Wyatt moved to the window and stared out at the activity with unmistakable longing. Sutton peered over his shoulder. "What game is that?"

"Flag football," he said, a wistful note lacing his words.

Remy sidled in beside her husband and bumped

shoulders. "How can you tell, baby? All I see is a lot of running around and snow being kicked up."

"Oh, it's definitely flag football," Wyatt said. "See, over there, the dead giveaway is poised in Casey's hand. And *that*, my friends, was a beautifully thrown spiral."

Sutton lifted on her toes for a better look. Sure enough, Casey had just launched a football in the air. McCoy caught the *beautifully thrown spiral* and took off running.

Wyatt sighed. The sound came out a little tortured and thoroughly miserable. Understandable. He'd been the star quarterback back in high school. And then again in college. He'd even played professionally, until he'd been forced to return home to raise his fifteen-year-old sister after their parents' boating accident.

Though Sutton would never say it out loud, football's loss was Thunder Ridge's gain. Wyatt was a dedicated lawman who kept their streets safe.

He sighed again.

Sutton decided to put the poor man out of his misery. "Mind if I hold Liam?"

The child was in her arms and Wyatt was halfway out the door before she finished the question. Reeling from the fast handoff, Sutton readjusted her hold on the baby, then took Wyatt's place next to Remy.

Together, they watched Wyatt trot over to Casey. The two men conversed for a moment, teams were reorganized, and then the game was back on.

"That was kind of you," Remy said, glancing at Sutton from the corner of her eye.

"Yes, very kind," Quinn said, moving to stand on Sutton's other side.

Flanked by the sisters, and more than a little uncomfortable, Sutton focused on the baby in her arms. "Don't be too impressed." She ran a fingertip along the curve of the smooth, plump cheek. "I miss holding a baby."

The other women agreed it was one of the best things in life.

"Wyatt's playing quarterback now," Remy announced. "And, oh, Sutton, look. Toby caught the ball."

Sutton watched her son tuck the football under his arm and run flat out across the snow-covered lawn. Casey kept pace with the boy, protecting him from the other players. Snow flew in their wake. Dogs barked. Grown men cried. And then…

Touchdown!

After a brief tutorial from Casey, Toby spiked the ball. Letting out a whoop, Casey swooped the boy in the air and spun him around in fast circles. Sutton's heart surged into her throat and stuck. The two looked so right together, so natural. She was still swallowing back an onslaught of emotions when Quinn's husband entered the kitchen and called out a greeting.

Welcoming the distraction, she turned away from the window. Grant Holloway looked every bit the high school principal that he was, from the tortoise-shell glasses, khaki pants and polished brown shoes to the button-down blue shirt beneath a dark-brown argyle sweater vest. He approached his wife. "Hello, gorgeous. Miss me?"

"Only every second you were away."

"Correct answer." He pulled her into his arms and placed a loud, smacking kiss on her lips. Quinn returned the gesture with impressive vigor for a woman wearing a baby on her front.

Sutton felt a twinge of momentary grief at the sight of all that marital bliss. If Jeremy were still alive, would he be inside kissing her? Or would he be outside playing flag football? None of the above. He'd be off somewhere top secret, barely communicating for weeks at a time.

She was being uncharitable. She'd always admired Jeremy's dedication to his job. The US Air Force had lost a good man. The world had lost a good man. And Toby had lost his father.

She glanced back out the window. The football game had been abandoned for sledding. Casey and Wyatt took turns loading kids onto sleds, while McCoy began building a snowman.

His dog danced around him, barking and eating clumps of snow he tossed in the air.

Eventually, the animal grew tired of the game and decided to steal Toby's ski cap. Casey shouted something. The dog danced to the left, then to the right, and that was all it took. The chase was on. Naturally, Toby was in the middle of the chaos.

Remembering her promise to her father, Sutton shifted the baby in her arms, dug her phone out of her pocket, then started snapping pictures with her free hand. No easy task.

"Let me help you with that." Quinn materialized by her side and took the phone. She turned it sideways and started snapping away. "My brother's always been good with kids."

They both knew she was talking about Casey. "Toby adores him."

Quinn nodded. Then, surprising them both, reached out and threw her arm over Sutton's shoulders. "It's great having you back in Thunder Ridge. Welcome home, girlfriend."

Warmth filled her. Simple, heartfelt words that bridged years of animosity. Sutton took a deep breath and spoke the truth in her heart. "Thank you, Quinn. It's good to be back."

Casey extracted Toby's ski cap from the jaws of one very large, very playful Saint Bernard. This was not his first ski cap rescue from the gentle giant, nor would it be his last. Bertha was big and clumsy. She was also sweet and relatively harmless, unless you were a piece of winter outerwear. No cap, glove, mitten, or freshly laundered sock was safe in her company. "Bad dog."

Bertha barked. Then sped off looking for another victim.

Now that he had possession of Toby's hat, Casey contemplated returning it to the little boy's head. The vast amount of dog slobber erased any chance of providing warmth against the cold temperatures. Not that Toby noticed. He was too busy asking questions about the car he and Casey were going to build. "Will I get to use a wrench?"

"Absolutely. In fact..." Casey stuffed the drenched ski cap in his back pocket. "You'll be doing most of the work."

"Really?" Toby's eyes widened to three sizes their normal size. "That's so cool. Can we start today? Like this afternoon? Maybe even right now?"

"Nope, sorry, kid." He gave the boy's shoulder a friendly squeeze. "Not right now. We'll start tomorrow after church."

Toby scrunched his face. "How come not today?"

"Because the rules require that all entrants build the exact same gravity-powered stock car." He gave the shoulder another squeeze. "Since I only found out about the derby this afternoon, I still have to buy the car from the AASBD website."

Toby looked confused. "But if everybody races the exact same cars, how does anybody win?"

"That is an excellent question. The deciding factor comes down to the skill of the driver, which is, in this case, you."

"Oh." The boy's face fell. "But I'm only seven. I don't know how to drive yet."

"That's where I come in." Casey tugged the kid into a one-arm hug. "I, my friend, am an excellent driver. I have seven Soap Box Derby trophies to prove it. I'm going to teach you everything I know."

"That sounds great." Toby rubbed at his chin, his eyes lit with excitement again. "This really is going to be fun."

"It really is."

"So…" Toby glanced over his shoulder. "Do you think there're any cupcakes left?"

Ah, the mind of a seven-year-old boy. From cars to cupcakes in 0.6 seconds. "Possibly. What do you say we head back inside and check it out for ourselves?"

"Let's do it." Toby took off toward the house.

Casey followed closely behind. Halfway across the lawn, he noticed Sutton watching their approach from the kitchen. She held a baby in her arms. She looked good. Incredible. Amazing. He couldn't take his eyes off her. His chest tightened, as it always did when his gaze caught hers. He kept walking, kept staring.

It was clear she was having her own moment of appreciation. With one big difference. She was looking at her son. Not Casey. How many hits could one man's ego take in a day?

Unaware his steps had slowed, Toby rushed inside the house ahead of Casey. When he stepped across the threshold, the little boy looked decidedly crushed. "I don't see any cupcakes."

Casey didn't, either. Nor did he see Sutton. She'd disappeared. Where had she gone?

"Hey, Mr. Casey." Toby pulled on his sleeve. "Did you bring Winston and Clementine with you? Because I could watch them for a while. If you want. They really like me."

This was true. Bulldogs were a friendly breed by nature, and naturally good with kids, but his matching pair had taken a special liking to Toby. Casey regretted not bringing them with him this afternoon. There had been reasons, which he explained now. "Winston had an early wake-up call. He's currently at home sleeping."

"What about Clementine and the puppies?" Toby gave Casey the hopeful smile that tugged at his heart every time. Every. Time.

He delivered the bad news with a stoic expression. "They are also at home. You'll get to see them tomorrow afternoon. When we start working on getting you ready for the derby."

"I guess that'll be okay." Now that the subject of puppies had been broached, Toby pressed on. "Have you found homes for all of them?"

"All but two."

"Really? You have two left?"

"Yep."

"A puppy would make a perfect Christmas present for a seven-year-old boy."

Casey did not disagree. However, as if on cue, Sutton came around the corner and squashed her son's hopes. "No puppy for Christmas, Toby. Not this year."

"Ah, come on, Mom. Two whole puppies are still available for adoption. Mr. Casey said so."

"Still no."

The boy remained undeterred. "But Samson got Roscoe last time, when it was supposed to be me getting one of the puppies because I did so well at Puppy School."

Casey hid his smile behind a cough. Sutton had stepped right into that one. Although she hadn't made any promises last summer, she'd suggested that if Toby took lessons on how to train a dog with his sister, Remy, she'd consider getting him a puppy. Casey had been there. He'd heard the entire conversation. Naturally, Toby had taken his mother's maybe and turned it into a yes.

"We've been through this before, Toby. I'm too busy to house-train a puppy right now. Maybe next time Clementine has puppies—"

"This is Clementine's final litter."

"What?" Sutton and Toby asked at the same time with Sutton adding, "Why?"

"Giving birth is hard on bulldogs," Casey explained with a deceptively careless shrug. "The first litter was difficult enough on Clementine. She barely survived the second one."

"Oh, Casey. I'm sorry." Sutton said, concern in her eyes. "I didn't know."

"She had to have a cesarean section." Casey wasn't putting his best girl through that again.

"But you have puppies left, right?" Toby persisted as only a kid on a mission to get his own puppy could. "So one of them could be mine? If my mom says it's okay?"

"Your mom says no," Sutton said before Casey could respond.

"But, Mom—"

"No, Toby. A puppy needs to be house-trained, which is especially hard in wintertime."

True, but this was another area where Casey excelled. He could help them out. For Toby's sake, of course. He was about to make the offer when a disembodied voice shouted to no one in particular. "When does the snowman competition begin?"

Another voice answered from a completely different part of the house. "Already started. And McCoy is winning by default since he's the only one actually building a snowman."

Grant sped out the backdoor, shouting, "Prepare to watch and learn, McCoy Evans. Watch and learn."

"Hey." Sutton rested a hand on Toby's shoulder. "Want to build a snowman?"

It was a valiant effort at distraction, and yet doomed to fail from the start. Toby hung his head. "Not really. I'd rather play with puppies."

"I know, baby. But maybe we could craft a little snow puppy for our snowman to hold."

"That would be kind of cool, I guess."

"It will be. Come on, kiddo. Let's give it our best shot."

"Okay, sure." Toby set out after his mom, dragging his feet at a third of the speed he usually applied to just about everything.

Sutton gave Casey a quick glance on her way out the door, then she was gone. He considered following her and Toby. It would be fun. His family took their snowmen seriously. They actually gave out awards. Back in the day, he and Sutton always entered as a team. They never won, usually because they ended up getting distracted by their own private snowball fight. Mostly started by Sutton, with Casey happily following her lead and…

He didn't finish the thought. It would only make him nostalgic. He didn't want to be nostalgic. He wandered into the living room instead and took in the Christmas decorations without really seeing them. His feet moved toward the front door, when an object snagged his eye. He froze, looked closer. On the mantel, mixed in with all the other photos, was a framed picture of him in the hospital, holding one of Remy and Wyatt's newborn babies.

Casey couldn't remember which one. He could, however, remember the joy that came from holding the infant. And then the accompanying spurt of envy that his youngest sister had managed to do what he hadn't been able to pull off himself. She'd made a baby. Make that *two* babies, who were about to experience their first Christmas with the family.

He tried to remain stoic. But he could feel his pulse quickening. His mind fought through a haze of what-ifs and "never will bes." The front door opened and closed, and he turned to see the batch of new arrivals. Casey's brother Walker was in the lead, hefting a diaper bag. Behind him, his wife, Hope, carried their toddler daughter.

Something clenched in Casey's gut at the sight

of his brother's smile. Walker had the look of a smitten parent. It was the same look Casey saw on Quinn's face whenever she gazed at her children. No different than the one on Remy's face nearly every moment of every day, or Wyatt's, or Grant's, or even his youngest brother's when Brent looked at his six-year-old twin daughters.

A baby boom had exploded in the Evans family. And it had happened without Casey or his brother McCoy. McCoy seemed in no hurry to join their siblings in parenthood. Casey, on the other hand, was years behind his own personal schedule. He should have at least two kids by now, with another on the way.

He had a good life, he reminded himself. Full of family, good friends, and two thriving, highly successful businesses. The thought only managed to annoy him.

His watch dinged, indicating an incoming call. He retrieved his cell phone, checked the caller ID, and said to the now-empty room, "I need to take this."

A minute later he was jogging out to his truck while also sending a group text to the family explaining his sudden departure. He was up in the air within the hour, flying toward Telluride to pick up a package that needed delivering to a small town in western Nebraska.

He didn't think about personal timelines during the flight. Or the babies he didn't have. He didn't think about Christmas, either. Or Sutton and her son. He only thought about transporting the package sitting in the back of his plane. When he finally arrived home, he spent the remainder of his waking hours channel surfing between two college football games.

The next morning, he arrived at Cargo Coffee only slightly refreshed but ready to tackle a busy day behind the espresso machine. One problem with his plan. A six-foot plastic Santa was already manning the controls. And if Casey wasn't mistaken, jolly Old Saint Nick winked at him.

Impressed with Sutton's ingenuity, he considered texting her a giant thumbs-up. Or maybe he should contact Wyatt and have her arrested for breaking and entering. Casey would graciously bail her out, eventually, in a day or two.

Then again, that would be petty.

On second thought, he would get even instead.

He had a few ideas, one that was downright genius—but would take time and possibly require assistance from a friend. Easy-peasy. Because, unlike a certain town mayor, Casey Evans was not above asking for help when the situation warranted.

Glancing at Santa, he decided the situation definitely warranted.

He pulled out his phone and went to work.

# Chapter Five

Sutton stood in her kitchen, head in the refrigerator, wishing she'd made a grocery run the night before. The limited offerings weren't a problem for her. She consumed the bulk of her calories in the afternoon. But Toby needed proper nourishment in the morning, particularly this one. He had a packed schedule, starting with Sunday school and ending with several hours at Casey's.

Initially, Sutton had balked at using Casey's garage as main headquarters for building Toby's derby car. She'd agreed only after a series of back-and-forth late-night texts. True, Casey's garage *was* larger and had the proper tools, but that hadn't been the reason she'd given in. Sutton had simply been too weary from recent events and the accompanying emotions to engage in yet another battle with Casey Evans.

Well, it was done now. No more second-guessing herself.

She made her decision about Toby's breakfast, grabbed the ingredients and closed the refrigerator door with her hip. Between cracking eggs and frying bacon, she slid frequent glances at her phone. Anticipation filled her. Casey should be arriving at Cargo Coffee any minute and discover the little surprise she'd arranged for him. Would he call or send a snarky text?

Her phone dinged. Ah, well, then. Text it was.

Adrenaline kicking in, she swiped her thumb across the screen and read the brief message. It's on.

Smiling, she considered sending an equally short reply. But she decided the situation warranted a longer response. She typed quickly, gave her message a quick review, made a small revision, then pressed Send. After I plied Santa with milk and cookies, he confessed he's always wanted to moonlight as a barista.

Casey's response came three seconds later. At the risk of bursting Santa's bubble, I recommend he stick to delivering presents. A barista he is not.

Sutton's laugh came quick and unexpected, sounding a little rusty even to her own ears.

"What's so funny, Mom?"

She grinned at her son who was currently standing too close to the hot stove. She gave him a gentle nudge back before saying, "I played a joke on Mr. Casey."

"What kind of joke?"

"A really funny one. Here. Take a look." She scrolled open the photos app on her phone, then turned the screen toward her son.

Toby squinted at the image. "I don't get it."

"Look closer. Right…there." She pointed to a spot in the center of the phone.

"Whoa. Is that the same Santa we found on our roof the other day?"

"It is, indeed." She let out another laugh. "I arranged for him to hang out at Cargo Coffee this morning. But if I know Mr. Casey—" which, of course, she did "—Santa will be back in my possession very soon."

Toby shook his head. "Adults are so weird."

"You won't get an argument from me." Still smiling, she kissed him on the head. "Ready to eat?"

"I was ready ten minutes ago."

She laughed. Her son had two great loves: food and puppies.

The rest of the morning seemed to pass at lightning speed. Sutton didn't see Casey at church, not that she'd expected him to show. Cargo Coffee was consistently busy on Sunday mornings, more so now that the holiday season was upon them. She did get a friendly wave from several members of his family, including Quinn, who added a smile that actually included her eyes. Sutton smiled back, a feeling of warmth spreading through her. Maybe, just maybe, she and Quinn could find their way back to being friends.

Sutton encountered Remy's husband outside Toby's Sunday school classroom. Wyatt stood in classic lawman pose, eyes level, arms crossed, gaze scanning the immediate area. Sutton had known the man nearly as long as she'd known Quinn and Casey. They'd always been friendly, but never really friends.

These days their paths crossed more often now that she was the mayor of their consolidated city-county and Wyatt was the elected sheriff. Still, other than organizing playdates for Samson and Toby they rarely interacted outside of work. Yesterday at Quinn's house had been a first.

She approached him with a smile. "Doesn't Remy usually pick up your nephew from Sunday school?"

Wyatt nodded. "The babies were fussy, so she took them home. It worked out since Samson and I need to pick up a few supplies so we can fine-tune his soapbox car."

"You're already fine-tuning his car?" Sutton couldn't keep the shock out of her voice.

"Don't be too impressed," Wyatt said. "We accomplished a lot on Thanksgiving Day. The cable went out."

Ah, that made sense. But if they were truly

that far along in the process, that meant Casey and Toby were behind schedule.

The door to the classroom swung open and out spilled a wave of seven-year-old boys and girls. Toby and Samson brought up the rear, their little heads bent in discussion. Sutton thought she heard the word *puppies* and tried not to sigh too loudly. Her son was on a mission.

She braced for the next phase of his I-want-a-puppy-for-Christmas campaign. He surprised her. "Guess what, Mom? Samson lost a tooth and the tooth fairy gave him five whole dollars."

"Five whole dollars? Wow." She eyed Wyatt. "Is that the going rate these days?"

He shrugged. "The tooth fairy is making up for lost time."

Meaning Remy had gone overboard in her role as surrogate mother to Samson. His real mother was serving time in prison for a felony drug charge, which had to be tough on the boy. "The tooth fairy is a very kind person."

Wyatt's smile spoke of his love for his wife. "She's also very generous."

They shared a laugh. Everyone said goodbye and went their separate ways.

After a quick lunch at the Latte Da diner, Sutton steered her car toward the edge of town. Toby carried most of the conversation on the way out to Casey's house. He covered the important topics of puppies, letters to Santa and what kind of lights he wanted on his Christmas tree. He circled back to puppies, then asked, "Want to know what we learned in Sunday school today?"

Thrown by the change of topic, Sutton caught her son's eye in the rearview mirror and smiled. "I absolutely do."

"We learned about gratitude."

"Pastor Stillwell covered the same topic in Big Church."

"Cool. Miss Montgomery said that if I want more yeses, and fewer noes, I need to say thank-you a lot more often. Sooo..." Toby lifted his chin and grinned at her via the mirror. "Thanks, Mom."

"For what?"

"For being the best mom ever!"

The day instantly became brighter. Sutton couldn't help the little sigh of pleasure that slipped out. "Aw, thanks, baby. And I think you're the best son ever."

He fell silent. Then, "If you wanted to give me a puppy for Christmas I'd say thank-you every day for the rest of my life."

And there it was. "Nice try, kiddo. But no puppy."

Toby was not to be deterred. "You're saying no, but I'm hearing maybe."

Sutton tried to keep a straight face. But could

her son be any more adorable? "*Maybe* I should call Dr. Bartlett and have your ears checked."

"You are so not funny, Mom."

She braked at a stop sign, then glanced over her shoulder. "I kind of thought I was."

"Okay, yeah. You are funny. Sometimes. Just not now." He turned away, looked out the window, sighed in resignation. "I'm still glad you're my mom."

"Even if I don't get you a puppy?"

Toby heaved another weighty sigh. "Even if you don't get me a puppy."

Soft ripples of affection slid through her. She turned back around and, after checking for traffic, accelerated through the intersection. "I love you, Toby Wentworth. With all my heart."

"Yeah, yeah. I know. I love you, too."

Heart full, she took the next turn. "What else do you want for Christmas?"

The list was long and detailed. Sutton took mental notes. Toby was winding down when she made the sharp right turn onto Casey's property.

The house nestled at the foot of the Rocky Mountains was gorgeous with lots of wood, river rock, and miles of glass to let in the view. It was also too big for a single male. Sutton could picture four or five kids running around the yard, dogs chasing after them. Add in that delicious overhanging roofline and the two covered wrap porches, and the place was a perfect setting for raising a large, happy family.

Except for one glaring flaw.

Casey had failed to hang a single Christmas decoration. Was the man trying to sabotage her efforts to win the contest? Or did he really hate Christmas that much? Either way, the magazine competition began in three days. One of the categories included exterior illumination, not only in the town proper, but also in the surrounding neighborhoods. Okay, technically, Casey's property was outside the county line. Just barely.

Frowning, Sutton continued onto the massive five-car garage constructed out of the same naturally treated wood and river rock as the house. She put the car in Park. Toby was already unbuckling his seat belt before she pulled the keys from the ignition. He climbed out the back seat a beat ahead of her and literally hit the ground running.

Sutton followed, envying her little boy's excitement as she glanced around.

Casey had parked his vintage pickup outside the garage. Another, newer truck sat beside it. Sutton recognized the cherry red Ford F-150. It belonged to her uncle on her mother's side. Horace Michaels had been the long-standing sheriff of Thunder Ridge until his retirement three years ago. He'd also been the first law enforcement officer on the scene the night of her eighteenth birthday party. He'd hauled Casey off to jail and had written up the charges himself.

Oddly, the two had remained close ever since the arrest.

Which begged the question, why? Why had Sutton's uncle kept close tabs on what he must have considered just another troublemaker in town? It wasn't as if Casey needed a father figure. His own was a good, godly man who'd remained present in his son's life long after his arrest.

Puzzled, she entered the garage and hesitated just inside the threshold, looking around, taking it all in. The interior was meticulously organized and surprisingly spotless. A row of lower cabinets and upper shelves lined the entire wall to her right. Several freestanding toolboxes stood close by, along with plastic containers of every shape and size filled with who knew what. On the left side of the building, stood the '63 Mustang and the GTO, both protected by car covers.

Clearly, Casey took care of what he owned. Impressed, her eyes sought and found the man himself. He wasn't alone; two other men flanked him. The rush of surprise stopped Sutton in her tracks. She'd expected to see her uncle, but it was the other man that gave her pause.

"Grandpa!" Toby skidded to a halt inches from slamming into Sutton's father. The older man flung out his arms and hugged the boy hard. Laughing, Toby spun around and hugged his uncle next, a man much shorter and stockier than Beau Fowler, with gravel-gray hair shorn in a military-style buzz cut.

"I didn't know you'd be here, too, Uncle Horace."

"What? And miss out on a chance to spend time with my favorite nephew? Never."

Laughing, Toby shot over to the third man in the building. "Hey, Mr. Casey."

"Hey, there, little man." Casey looked relaxed and supremely confident, a man who was thinking five steps ahead of everyone else. But then Toby hugged him, and his composure broke for a fraction of a second. A man momentarily lost and slightly unmoored, but the impression was gone in the next instant, replaced with his typical swagger.

"Ready to get started?" he asked.

"You bet I am. But…" Toby glanced to his left, then to his right, then left again. "Where's Winston and Clementine? And, you know…" more searching "…the puppies?"

"All dogs are inside the house, safely away from working tools and flying debris."

"Oh, yeah, smart. So…" Toby scuffed his foot. "Do you think I could maybe play with them later, if there's time?"

"I don't see why not." Casey slung an arm over

the boy's shoulders. "Come take a look at what your grandfather came up with for the outside of your car."

As Sutton watched the three men and one very happy little boy hunch over a worktable, a wash of gratitude swept through her. Casey had done this for her son. He'd invited Toby's grandfather and uncle, thereby turning the Soap Box Derby into a family affair. Touched by his thoughtfulness, she breathed the whole scene in, while an unsettling sensation surrounded her heart. Why hadn't Casey asked her to join in the fun?

As if sensing her eyes on him, he looked up. She stepped into view. Frowning, he cut his eyes from Toby, then glanced back to her. Holding her gaze, he said something to the boy and began his approach across the garage, stopping at a respectable distance.

Sutton must have smiled because a slow grin spread across Casey's face. "Hey."

Oh, boy. One word, spoken in that low, husky voice, and she was seventeen again, caught in the thrill of first love. "Hey, Casey."

"You just dropping off the boy or do you plan on sticking around?"

Sutton's throat tightened. Was he being polite? Or was he asking her to stay? "I'm heading out. I have work waiting for me back at the office."

It was true. The magazine contest officially

began in three days, which happily coincided with Thunder Ridge's first official Christmas event of the season. The tree-lighting ceremony was always well attended.

A muscle bunched in Casey's jaw. "Of course you have work waiting for you. Don't know why I would think otherwise."

She'd disappointed him—that much was clear. She wanted to change her answer, and maybe erase the censure off his face, but she couldn't seem to make herself say the words. "I guess I better get going."

"I guess you better." He added a small, humorless smile. Another clue she'd failed some sort of test. Which was absurd. Surely, Casey wasn't testing her. What would be the point?

And why did she have to overthink everything? Why couldn't she just act like a normal person around the man? Because this was Casey. They'd shared a past that had ended abruptly. There hadn't been any real closure, at least not for her.

She blinked hard, fearing tears would spring to her eyes if she didn't. It wasn't Casey's words, or even his tone that hurt. It was the invisible wall he'd erected between them. He might as well have said, *Bye, Sutton. Run along. You aren't needed here*.

No, he didn't say the words, but it was clear he

wanted her gone. So, of course, she stood rooted to the spot, head high, shoulders back, standing her ground as if she had nothing better to do than engage in a wordless battle.

Casey waited for Sutton to turn and leave his garage. She did neither, clearly expecting him to make the next move. He bristled, ready to engage in the standoff, until he noted the hint of heartache in her gaze and the twinge of some other emotion that bordered on hurt.

Her lips flattened to a thin line, her eyes blinking rapidly.

Was she about to cry? No, not that, *anything* but that. Casey was useless against female tears, especially when the woman shedding said tears was Sutton. Unable to stop himself, he lifted his hand toward her face, wanting to offer comfort.

She stepped out of his reach. "Anyway." She took a careful, measured breath. "What time should I pick up Toby?"

Letting his hand drop, he continued studying her face. Something there. Something that had nothing to do with him, or maybe it had everything to do with him. He'd upset her somehow. "No need to come all the way back out here. I'll bring Toby to you. Let's say around…five, six?"

She wanted to argue. Casey could see it in eyes. She wanted to tell him she didn't need anything from him, not one single thing, but she seemed to pull herself together and nodded her agreement. "Either time works. Just text me which."

"Let's say closer to six."

"Fine." She turned to go, then spun back around as if suddenly remembering some new offense he'd wrought against humanity. "I noticed you haven't decorated your house for Christmas."

And there it was, the accusation. The battle lines drawn. He would not take the bait. He gave her a blank look, one he hoped showed zero indication of what he was thinking. Not that he knew himself. The woman made his head spin. "You do realize I live outside the county line."

Her eyes flashed fire. "I'm aware. That's still no excuse. If it's a matter of time—"

"It's not."

"—I can help you with the basics, or whatever you need, depending on—"

"Do *not* finish that sentence. I mean it, Sutton. I refuse to discuss this any further."

Huffing out a breath, she folded her arms across her waist. "Why are you so resistant to hanging a few twinkling lights and a couple strands of garland?"

Casey fought the instinct to sigh. He didn't need to explain himself. Not to Sutton. Not to anyone. "What I do or don't do on my property is nobody's concern."

"Wow, Remy was right. You really are Ebenezer Grinch."

"Sticks and stones, Sutton. Sticks and stones."

She chewed on that a moment, then came at him from a different angle. "I admit, you are correct. You do live outside the county line. *However*—" she raised a hand to prevent him from interrupting "—the judges won't know that."

"So tell them."

"You know I can't do that."

He knew no such thing. "Why not?"

"Because..." she said, drawing out the word, "the judges' identities are supposed to remain secret. Assuming I could even figure out who they are, the act of pulling them aside and explaining your determination to win Scrooge of the Year would basically amount to cheating."

"And cheating would, of course, be wrong?" It was a rhetorical question. Of course, he knew cheating was wrong.

"Yes, Casey. Cheating would be wrong. Enormously inappropriate."

"Tremendously inappropriate," he agreed, his humor returning the more she fumed. "Mammoth, colossal. Ginormous."

"What's with all the clever adjectives? You bought yourself a thesaurus recently?"

"I have a word-of-the-day calendar in my office. Comes in handy when talking to you."

Sutton sort of smiled, a little, if he angled his head slightly to the left and squinted real hard. Yep, there it was. A slight twitch of her lips. "This conversation is far from over, Casey. You know that, right? I won't quit pestering you until you cave."

Casey Evans never caved. "Wow, Sutton, you're as tenacious as Winston with a bone, or Clementine with my favorite slipper."

"Very funny. We'll table this discussion for now." She sounded very mayoral. "To be revisited at another time and place convenient for us both."

"December twenty-sixth works for me. You free that day?"

She did smile then, but only a bit. "We'll try again tomorrow. Tuesday at the latest. Meanwhile, I'm gone."

She trotted out to her car without a single glance back in his direction.

He called after her. "Bye, Sutton."

Nothing.

"Always a pleasure talking with you."

Still nothing.

"See you at six o'clock."

Finally, she gave a short little wave over her head before ducking inside her car. He was watching her execute a spectacular three-point turn when Toby came up beside him. "Grandpa and Uncle Horace want to know what we should be working on right now."

"We should probably read through the rules."

Toby made a face. "Ugh, that sounds really, really boring."

"But also really, really necessary. The faster we get to it, the sooner we can tackle the fun stuff."

"I like that idea."

It took ten minutes to read through the rules. "According to this footnote," Casey said, "the combined weight of the assembled car and driver shall not exceed two hundred pounds. How much do you weigh, kid?"

"I don't know."

"Hmm, let's find out." He picked up the boy with one arm, the move earning him a series of happy seven-year-old squeals of delight. "I say you're maybe just shy of fifty pounds."

"Is that too much?"

"Nope." He set the laughing kid back on the ground. "All good."

Horace and Beau laughed. Toby grinned. "So, is it time for tools now?"

"Not yet. We need to make sure we have all the right ones first." Computer screen open, Casey consulted the list provided by the All-American Soap Box Derby organization, then rummaged in the drawers of a freestanding tool chest. He called out the name of each tool as he set it on the counter. "Screwdriver, wrench, socket, pliers, measuring tape, hammer, C-clamp, drill, drill bits, and..." he reached into a different drawer "...electrical tape."

Toby surveyed the pile. "That's a lot of hardware."

"Building a gravity-powered car is a big project." Casey gave Horace and Beau the task of grabbing two more sets of every tool, explaining to Toby, "Never hurts to be overprepared."

As the two men went to work, Toby hung close to Casey. Something on the wall caught his eye. "Hey, Mr. Casey, is that you?"

Casey followed the direction of the boy's gaze, straight to a picture of him standing in front of his F-22 Raptor. His hair was regulation short, and he was dressed in full flight gear, feet spread, one hand on a hip, the other holding his helmet. "Yep, that's me."

"I have a picture just like that of my dad. I keep it next to my bed." Toby's face glowed with pride and a hint of sadness. "Dad is standing in the exact same pose, except he has a helicopter behind him."

Casey battled a fresh wave of grief. "Your dad was one of the best pilots in the entire United States Air Force."

"Really? Wow." Toby swung around, eyes big and round. "I forgot you knew my dad."

The grief came again, bathing Casey in something cold and terrible. Some things couldn't, *shouldn't* be brushed off, even if it hurt to talk about them. "I knew him well. We were best friends as kids."

"Like me and Samson?"

"Exactly like you and Samson. Here. Take a look at this." Casey reached up and removed a different photograph from the wall. "This was taken right after my first Soap Box Derby. That's me." He placed his finger on the image of his seven-year-old self, mugging for the camera. "And that's your dad."

"His trophy is bigger than yours."

Casey chuckled. "That's because he won the race that day. I came in second."

Toby nodded, as if this made perfect sense to his seven-year-old brain. "Know what, Mr. Casey? I'm going to beat Samson, just like my dad beat you."

"That, little man, is the plan."

# Chapter Six

The morning of the tree-lighting ceremony dawned sunny and crisp, with temperatures in the low twenties and winds less than five mph. The forecast looked promising for the next twenty-four hours. Sutton prayed the weather held. In the meantime, she had a dozen details to finalize. The amount was nothing short of daunting.

*One task at a time.*

After dropping Toby off at school, she spent the first hour of her workday reviewing the evening's schedule of events with her assistant. Maria Torres was young and hungry for advancement, as Sutton had been at her age. "I'll follow up with the event coordinator about the additional outdoor speakers you requested," Maria said. "Is there anything else you want me to run by her?"

"Nothing I can think of. Oh, except let her know I'll be available for a sound check within the hour, or any time after that."

Maria made a notation on her phone. "Got it. Anything else?"

"I think we're good."

Sutton's next stop was the sheriff's office. Wyatt's administrative assistant, Doris, met her at the door, all but barring her entrance into the building. The older woman's steely gray eyes were narrowed beneath a head of wiry hair the color of a hawk's muted silver-brown. It was no secret Doris ran the sheriff's office with a no-nonsense, by-the-book commitment to order. She had zero tolerance for shenanigans—her word—no sense of humor that Sutton had ever noticed, and guarded Wyatt's schedule like Clementine watched over her puppies.

The woman was scary with a capital S.

She was also currently sweeping a long, assessing glance over Sutton with her hallmark efficiency. She did not look happy. Of course, Doris rarely looked happy. Sutton lifted her chin and put a good dose of authority in her voice. "I need to speak with Sheriff Holcomb."

"His calendar is full this morning."

Sutton already knew this. "I only need five minutes. Seven at the most."

"No can do. Sheriff Holcomb—"

"—can spare five minutes for his boss," Wyatt said from the threshold of his office. "Come on in, Sutton."

She did as the man requested, ignoring how Doris's eyes flickered with annoyance as she passed by the older woman. "Thanks for fitting me in on such short notice."

"No problem." He sat behind his desk, then indicated she take one of the two chairs facing him. "Have a seat."

"Thanks, but I'll stand." At his questioning stare, she added, "This really will only take five minutes."

"All right." He leaned back in his chair. "What can I do for you?"

"Where are we on crowd control for tonight?"

"My deputies will cover the bulk of the duties." He laid out the specifics, then added, "I also asked three of our neighbors for additional help. All but one answered my call."

"Which one? No, don't tell me." She held up a hand. "Village Green is the lone holdout."

"Affirmative."

Sutton wasn't surprised. Village Green was thirty miles west of Thunder Ridge and took the holiday season seriously. By all accounts, their closest neighbor was also their stiffest competition. "I guess it's true what they say. All's fair in love, war and a national magazine contest."

"Is that what they say?"

"Am I wrong?"

Wyatt laughed. "No, ma'am. Set your mind

at ease, Sutton. I have more than enough deputies scheduled for duty tonight." He rose from his chair and rounded the desk. "You can tick crowd control off your list and move on to the next item."

"Thank you, Wyatt. See you tonight. You, too, Doris," she said as she breezed by the still-scowling woman.

Outside on the sidewalk, Sutton retrieved her phone and crafted a quick text message to Thunder Ridge's resident celebrity, Reno Miller. The former professional skier had won every major downhill race. He also had a slew of world championships to his name and had graced covers of popular sports magazines. Some of the news outlets called him a national treasure. Others claimed he was the Bad Boy of the Slopes. Sutton figured the man fell somewhere in between. She also considered him a successful Thunder Ridge business owner and a good friend since high school.

She sent the text. Meet me at the Gazebo in twenty minutes.

Seconds later, Reno responded with a thumbs-up emoji.

With the sun bright and the wind practically nonexistent, Sutton chose to walk the two and a half blocks, taking in the decorations, the freshly fallen snow, the buildings covered in garland and multicolored lights. She paused to talk to several residents along the way, answering questions, posing a few of her own, waving to a teller from the bank, a clerk in her favorite store—the Ooh La La Boutique.

With each step she tried to picture Thunder Ridge through the eyes of a contest judge and saw, with no small amount of pride, a pristine town all dressed up for Christmas. Checking her watch, she realized what should have been a five-minute walk had turned into fifteen. She moved her feet faster, buzzing past the makeshift booths where local artisans and vendors were already setting up their temporary shops for the Christmas Market. Volunteers were setting up over five thousand candlelit luminaries that would light up the streets and sidewalks once the sun went down. Or what Sutton considered the most beautiful and romantic vision of the season.

The life-size Nativity scene looked picture-perfect nestled up against a clump of evergreens. At first glance, the handcrafted stable could pass for the real thing. The statue of Mary was very lifelike. Same for Joseph. Baby Jesus in His manger. The angels were also spot-on, as were the shepherds. The donkeys. Sheep.

Best of all, the wise men were a treat for the eye, resplendent in their satin robes, velvet tunics, corded belts and elaborate headdresses. Sutton absently counted them off as she walked past. One, two, three, four. *Four?*

Her feet ground to a halt.

Her mouth dropped open.

Her hands balled into fists. "That is just wrong."

On so many, many levels. Perched between the first wise man and the second, and attired in a blue-velvet tunic, gold crown and matching belt, stood the hideously tacky, six-foot Santa.

Sutton whipped out her phone. She swiped open the last text from Casey and let her thumbs dance the rumba across the screen. She paused, read her question—Explain this please—deleted the *please*, then pressed Send. She took a picture of the rogue Nativity member. Then sent that, as well.

Her phone immediately vibrated with an incoming call.

Casey was already talking before she said hello. "You are looking at what is called a Nativity scene, also known as a three-dimensional depiction of the birth of Jesus. Gee, Sutton, seeing as we attend the same church, I'm surprised you don't know that."

"I'm perfectly aware what a Nativity scene is. I'm also aware that a plastic Santa Claus does not belong in, around, or anywhere near one."

"Have a heart, will ya? After I fired him from his job as a barista, Santa wanted redemption. At his age, he's far more suited for the role of wise man than a shepherd boy."

"Not funny, Casey." She commandeered the plastic offender and looked around for a place to stash him temporarily. She chose the bushy evergreen tree closest to her. "Really not funny."

"Then why are you smiling?"

"You can't possibly know if I'm smiling or not." Or could he? She spun in a fast circle, looking for the man's large, annoying form. He could be anywhere. Behind a building, a tree, a Nativity scene. "Are you spying on me?"

"I'm wounded you would even ask." He didn't sound wounded. He sounded amused.

Feeling like a guppy swimming around in a fishbowl, she circled the general area. Looked left, right. No Casey. "Where are you?"

"In my car, heading down Highway 63."

Which explained the tinny reverb that made his voice sound like it was coming at her through a small ocean. "Well, you can turn yourself around and come get Santa. He's beneath one of the trees behind the Nativity scene."

"You just dumped Santa in the trees?"

"Yes," she said, growling out the word. "Oh, yes, I did. You got a problem with that, Evans?"

"Kind of touchy, aren't we, Sutton?"

"It's been a long day," she said before she could censor her words, hating how tired she sounded, and that she felt safe enough to let him hear her exhaustion.

"It's barely nine o'clock in the morning."

"Stop playing games, Casey. This isn't the time or the place."

"You're right."

"Of course, I'm right. Putting the plastic Santa Claus in the Nativity scene was wrong and irreverent." She pitched her voice to a husky baritone that mimicked his. "Gee, Casey, seeing as we attend the same church, I'm surprised you don't know that."

"I'll say again, you're absolutely right. I crossed a line." His voice held a serious note that spoke of genuine remorse. "I had second thoughts almost immediately. In fact, I was already on my way to fetch Santa when your text came through."

She sighed. "Let's pretend I believe you."

His chuckle did strange things to her stomach. "If it makes you feel any better, Santa was a part of the Nativity scene for barely fifteen minutes."

She said nothing.

It was his turn to sigh. "I really did have a change of heart. In fact, I'm only a few blocks away from where you're standing."

So he said. "Goodbye, Casey. I'm hanging up now."

He barely got her name out before she pressed the red icon on her screen and the phone went dead. Very satisfying. Hands on hips, she eye-balled the plastic monstrosity tangled in the blue tunic of a wise man. Matters had gotten out of hand. It was time to end this ridiculous war with Casey. One of them needed to act like an adult. Might as well be her. "You, my friend, are headed for the trash heap."

She bent down, placed her hands on his feet. The sound of a masculine chuckle had her letting go and whipping around. "Casey Evans, you are—Oh! Reno. Sorry. I thought you were someone else."

Reno's eyes twinkled with amusement. "So I gathered."

Flashing a toothy grin, he closed the distance, his steps that of a natural-born athlete. No doubt about it, the man was astonishingly good-looking in that Colorado skier sort of way, with his tall, rangy build and sun-kissed light brown hair. The contest judges were going to love him when he took the stage tonight. "Thanks for meeting me, Reno." They shook hands. "I hope I didn't pull you away from anything too important."

"Nothing that couldn't wait. What's up?"

"I want to run through the ceremony one final time before tonight."

He spread his arms. "I'm at your disposal for the rest of the morning."

"Twenty minutes is all I need. Follow me." As

she made a mental note to swing back around for Santa—no way did she believe Casey was heading back to town—she led Reno to the temporary stage next to the fifty-foot Christmas tree.

Phoebe Foxe, Wyatt's newest hire in the sheriff's department, stood nearby in a group of five other deputies. There was a fierce splendor to the woman, striking even in the unflattering forest green uniform. The female version of Reno, she was tall, with short, spikey black hair, and had the lithe, toned movements of an athlete.

Sutton had formed a tentative friendship with the sheriff's deputy, most of the effort on her side. A former detective for the Denver PD, Phoebe wasn't easy to get to know. To say she was guarded would be an understatement. But once she let down that guard, she was a lot of fun.

Seeing Sutton, Phoebe waved, then broke away from her fellow deputies. "I was about to text you. I have something I want to run by you before tonight. Can you spare a few minutes?"

"Sure, as soon as I'm through with Reno." She made the introductions. "Reno, this is Deputy Phoebe Foxe. Deputy Foxe, this is Reno Miller."

"We know each other," the two said in tandem. Only then did Sutton remember Phoebe had also been a professional snowboarder before switching to law enforcement.

From the glare Phoebe shot Reno, it was clear

she wasn't a fan of the Bad Boy of the Slopes. His stony silence indicated a mutual wariness. There was a story there, and maybe some bad blood, but Sutton was on a tight schedule. No time for a Q&A session.

"Once you and I take the stage," she said to Reno, "I'll start the ceremony with a brief welcome. I'll follow that with an even briefer speech, then introduce you. Once the thundering applause dies down—"

Phoebe snorted.

"—I'll hand you this." Sutton bent down and picked up the external remote switch the technicians had built for the sake of the audience. "And you'll make a grand show of turning on the lights. Any questions?"

Reno had none. Or maybe he did, hard to tell since he wasn't looking at her. He was too busy staring at Phoebe and not in that flirty, Reno way that had earned him his bad boy moniker. That was some serious tension in his shoulders. "Did you just snort?" he asked the deputy.

Phoebe made a vague gesture with her hand. "Thundering applause for you, Reno?" Her derision threaded through every word. "Do the people in this town actually know who you are?"

"What's your problem with me? It's not like I ever— Wait. Hold up. Just hold up a second. Is this about that night in Telluride? When we—"

"Stop right there."

He opened his mouth to continue. "Look, Phoebe, I know I—"

She cut him off. "Not another word, Reno. This is not the time to talk about that night."

"Why not?"

"You know why not?"

His shoulders lifted in a lazy shrug. "Not a clue."

She snorted again.

Feeling like an intruder, Sutton said, "I'll just give you two a few minutes."

Neither acknowledged her. Her frown deepened when she spotted Casey's '63 Mustang pull into the only empty parking space on the block. From behind the steering wheel, he hit her with the full force of his gaze. *Boom.* Her heart actually went boom. Inexplicably drawn to him, she started forward, hesitated, then pulled back like a woman avoiding a fall off a cliff. This sudden, vivid awareness of him worried her.

Okay, maybe not so sudden. He'd once touched the deepest chambers of her heart and left her hurting. She'd been young and naive back then. She was wiser now, smarter. So why couldn't she look away. Why couldn't he?

Still holding her gaze, Casey climbed out of his car. Something quite lovely bloomed in her heart, but she denied it, shoved it aside. Broke eye contact. When she looked up again, Casey was setting one of his bulldogs on the ground and snapping a leash to his harness. Winston. She immediately recognized the animal by the markings on his sweet, smushed-in face.

What she didn't recognize was Winston's ensemble. The dog wore a bright red sweater and matching booties on his feet. Atop his head sat—Sutton narrowed her eyes—was that reindeer antlers? A dozen uncharitable thoughts ran through her mind. Needing a moment to calm her temper, she took Winston's face in her hands and gave the dog a smacking kiss on his wrinkled cheek.

She straightened, jammed her hands on her hips, and faced his owner. "Let's see if I have this right. You won't hang a single strand of lights on your house, *or* your place of business, but you'll decorate your dog for Christmas?"

"Putting Winston in a red sweater does not constitute *decorating* him for Christmas."

"What about the matching booties?"

"His feet were cold."

She swallowed a snarky retort. "And the antlers?"

Casey looked down. "Huh, where did those come from?" Looking mildly appalled, he carefully snatched the festive headgear off the dog's head, then tossed the antlers in a nearby garbage can. "There, all better."

Reaching for a calm she didn't feel, Sutton lowered to her haunches again and cupped the dog's face. "Your daddy is a very frustrating, annoying man. But you, Winston Churchill Evans, are adorable. What do you say we run off together?"

"Careful, Sutton. Clementine is a jealous woman."

"Good thing she's not here to witness my shameful attempt to steal her man." She dropped a kiss to Winston's head, then stood again. *Take a breath, Sutton.* "Are you coming to the tree-lighting ceremony tonight?"

Casey didn't respond. He, like Reno earlier, was looking beyond her. She glanced over her shoulder. Oh, boy. Reno and Phoebe were arguing now, both gesturing wildly with their hands. "Wonder what that's about?" she asked aloud.

"No idea."

Reno pointed a finger at Phoebe. Phoebe pointed right back. More gesturing. More arguing. Then Phoebe threw her hands up in obvious frustration. Reno followed suit. The next instant, they were both storming off in opposite directions.

*That can't be good.* "I'm going after Phoebe," she said, already on the move.

Casey matched her step for step, his dog happily keeping pace. "Winston and I will take Reno."

Sutton caught up with her friend on the other side of the Gazebo. "Phoebe. Hey, Phoebe. Slow down. Please, I want to talk to you."

Without breaking stride, the woman glanced in her direction. "Not now, Sutton."

"I need to make sure you're okay."

Phoebe's steps slowed, then stopped altogether. She closed her eyes, rolled her shoulders as if shrugging off something uncomfortable, but nothing could erase the devastated look on her face. "Reno and I…" She opened her eyes and drew in a long, tortured breath. "We have a history."

"Yeah, there's a lot of that going around." Unable to help herself, Sutton glanced again in Casey's direction. He'd caught up with Reno, who didn't look any happier than Phoebe. Maybe even more upset. Sutton glanced at her friend again. "Want to talk about it?"

"No." The word came out watery and Phoebe's eyes shone with tears she kept from falling with fast, hard blinks.

"I'm a really good listener."

"I…it's…" She shook her head. "It's complicated."

Sutton felt a lump rise in her throat. "I know all about complicated histories." She glanced at Casey again.

That got a snicker out of Phoebe and a quick,

fleeting grin as she, too, looked in Casey's direction. "No doubt."

They both fell silent, each lost in their own thoughts.

"Anyway…" Phoebe said, breaking the silence first. "While I have your attention, I'd like to point out a few potential problem areas if the crowds get too large tonight. One over here on the north side of the Gazebo, the other a block over."

"What do you mean by problem areas?"

"Congestion, possible bottlenecks. We may want to think about adding barricades to keep the foot traffic moving. Or possibly another solution that would add a holiday feel and still get the job done. I have a few ideas."

Relieved to focus on work, Sutton embraced the change of subject. "Tell me what you have in mind."

After five minutes of attempting to pry information out of a close-lipped Reno, Casey decided communing with a brick wall would have been more productive. His friend wasn't giving up any of his deepest, darkest secrets. At least not where Phoebe Foxe was concerned. Because Casey could empathize—boy, could he ever—he respected his friend's privacy and went about his own business of the day, namely a delivery to a private airfield just outside Denver.

He made the short flight with his mind working out his next Santa prank. Sutton had forgotten to retrieve the poor old guy from behind the Nativity scene. Her mistake was Casey's opportunity to give the plastic monstrosity one final hurrah before retiring him from active duty. The game had gone on too long. Tonight would be Santa's last public appearance.

In the meantime, Casey had a little girl to make deliriously happy. He hoisted the dog carrier out of the cargo hold and sauntered toward the airport terminal, which was being kind. The metal shack was barely large enough to fit three people inside, possibly four if everyone held their breath.

Before he got a chance to test his theory, a little tow-headed girl around Toby's age came flying out of the building, arms waving, high-pitched squeals accompanying her every step. "Is that her? Is that my new puppy?"

Playing along, Casey presented the carrier as if she were royalty and he her lowly servant. "May she bring you much joy and happiness for many years to come."

When he set the carrier on the ground, the little girl dropped to her knees and peered past the wire door. "Aw, she's so cute."

"The cutest," her mother agreed as she drew alongside her daughter and offered Casey her hand. "Thank you for coming to us, Mr. Evans. My husband and I are grateful you made this so easy."

Casey could point out that they'd paid him handsomely for the hand delivery. But said, instead, "My pleasure."

Back in Thunder Ridge, he made one more puppy delivery to a local family. That made two down, one to go, with the final baby bulldog temporarily reserved for Toby. Either the kid would wear down his mother before Christmas, or Casey would. Every young boy should have his own dog.

After a fifteen-minute power nap, and an aggravating tug-of-war with Clementine over his shoe, he headed back into town to cover a late shift at Cargo Coffee.

With the tree-lighting ceremony still two hours away, business was, once again, booming. Casey served at least a hundred lattes in the first thirty minutes of his shift. The crowd eventually dwindled to the size of a small army. Then slowed to a steady stream. When there was nothing left but a few stragglers, he gathered his employees together for a brief team meeting. "And that," he told them, "is a wrap. Everybody out."

This earned him five identical expressions of confusion. "Apparently, I wasn't clear. Go on. Get out of here." He made a rolling motion with his hand. "The tree-lighting ceremony will be starting soon."

One of the newer employees took her cue. "You don't have to tell me twice."

Actually, that was exactly what he'd had to do. Nevertheless, a mass exodus ensued, minus one lone holdout. Emory Anderson, his manager and one of Remy's best friends. "I don't feel right leaving you like this," she said. "What if you get slammed again?"

"Not with Quinn's Sweet Shop supplying free hot chocolate and coffee out on the plaza. Seriously, Emory," he added when she opened her mouth to argue, "if I need your help, I'll text you. Now get out of here before I change my mind."

Her feet remained firmly planted in place, her mouth smiling. "Remy is wrong about you. You're not an Ebenezer Grinch. Not by a long shot."

He shouldn't respond. Best to let it go. It was the wise thing to do. The smart thing. And yet, he found himself asking, "When did she say that?"

"Last week. But like I said, she's wrong. You're no Scrooge. You're Frosty, Rudolph and Buddy the Elf all wrapped up in one big, sweet, Christmas-loving nice guy."

Not as offended as he should be, Casey put on a frown and pointed a finger in her general direction. "Take that back, Emory. Take it back right now."

"No can do. Admit it, Casey. You're a good guy underneath all that bluster." She patted his arm. "Best boss ever."

He magnified the frown, added a little eyebrow for good measure. "I hear the Latte Da is looking for a manager with your particular skill set."

"Nice try, but we both know this place would fall apart without me and my skill set."

"You are not wrong."

"I know. I also know how to graciously receive an unexpected gift. So, I'm out of here." She reached for the door, paused, looked back. "I'll check in later, okay?"

"Sounds good."

Over the next ten minutes, he served three more customers. Then he was alone with nothing but the echo of his footsteps as he cruised around the interior of the shop. At the large, plate glass window, he glared at his scowling reflection staring back at him. The look in his eyes was startling, black in the dim light, a bit hollow and full of misery. He'd been wearing that expression a lot since Victoria left, less often since Sutton marched into his shop with her ultimatums. So why the discontent now? He should be wildly happy. He was right where he wanted to be, away from all that sickly-sweet laughter and holiday cheer.

*Keep telling yourself that, Evans.*

He returned to his spot behind the counter. Another fifteen minutes passed with the grand total of zero customers entering the building, which was probably why he found himself at the window again. This time, he ignored his reflection and focused on the activity outside. Yep, a lot of laughter and holiday cheer.

It didn't take him long to locate Sutton among the blur of bodies. She stood in the town square near the fifty-foot Christmas tree. His breath caught in his throat at the sight she made in a pair of black jeans, black ankle boots, and a black, fitted puffer coat belted at the waist. She'd added color to the outfit with a bright red scarf and matching cap she'd placed at a jaunty angle atop her head.

She looked beautiful, elegant and classy, and every bit the woman in charge. He'd always liked that about her, how she moved through the world with purpose. So sure of herself. And Casey couldn't take his eyes off her. Sutton had always affected him like this, for as long as he'd known her, as children, preteens, then as teenagers. He remembered leaning lazily against the hood of his car in the high school parking lot and watching Sutton. He remembered walking through the halls from class to class and watching Sutton. Sitting in Chemistry, English, American History—and watching Sutton.

Some things, apparently, never changed.

Except tonight, Toby stood beside her, looking bored among all those adults. Before Casey realized what he was doing, he was shutting off lights, powering down computers, locking doors and joining the mass of humanity on the crowded sidewalk. He had one destination in mind.

Was it the right move? He had a moment of indecision and almost turned back. Then two distinct words filled his mind. *Why not?* Why not be with the people he cared about most?

As he moved closer to mother and son, he realized they weren't alone. Reno was there, entertaining the assembled crowd with his usual animated charm. Clearly, the man had recovered from his altercation with Phoebe Foxe. Casey approached, shouldering Reno aside so he could stand next to Sutton. "This guy bothering you?"

"Casey, I…you're here." The way Sutton's eyes lit up when they landed on his face gave his gut a hard kick. "I thought you weren't joining in the festivities tonight."

"I changed my mind." He nearly added, *I couldn't stay away from my two favorite people*, but caught himself.

Her smile widened. "I'm glad."

Pleasure spread through him. "Me, too." He glanced around. "Tell me how I can help."

"Everything's done. All you need to do is mingle and enjoy yourself."

Being close to her and Toby was all he needed. There was a growing tenderness in him he'd never fully explored with any other woman, not even the younger Sutton. Before he did something stupid, like break out in song, or recite catchy iambic pentameter, he dropped his gaze to Toby. "How's it going, little man?"

The boy pounced on the question like Clementine to one of Casey's shoes. "I'm super bored. My mom says I have to stay with her until Samson and Miss Remy show up."

In that, at least, Casey could offer some assistance. He glanced back at Sutton. "If it's okay with you, Toby can hang with me until my sister arrives."

"Can I, Mom? Can I hang with Mr. Casey?"

He expected an immediate no, possibly followed by a long-winded explanation as to all the reasons why. But Sutton's face relaxed into a smile and she said, "That's a lovely idea."

Casey didn't know who was more surprised by her easy acquiescence, him or Toby. Or possibly Sutton herself. He almost asked for an interpreter in case he'd misunderstood, then decided to follow his manager's lead and graciously receive this unexpected gift. "We'll stick close to the square," he told her. "No farther than Quinn's booth."

"That works for me." She looked about to say more but someone called her name and Toby was tugging on Casey's arm, and the next thing he knew they were going their separate ways with a muttered promise to meet up again later.

# Chapter Seven

After answering her assistant's question about lighting the luminaries, Sutton looked back over her shoulder. She shifted slightly so she could watch, uninterrupted, as Casey led Toby through the thickening crowd. He had one hand on the boy's shoulder in a protective gesture reminiscent of a father with his son. They looked so comfortable together, so right. Sutton stood frozen in the moment, helpless, wanting to weep. Out of joy or guilt? She didn't know which.

Tears wiggled to the edges of her eyes. She refused to let them fall. The accompanying emotion was harder to deny. She couldn't help thinking Jeremy should be the one guiding their son toward the Christmas Market. And yet, she wasn't sorry to see Toby growing closer to Casey. He was proving to be a good role model, and the boy was positively in awe of the man. Sutton knew the feeling. For months, she'd fought her attraction, convincing herself he couldn't be trusted. She had proof, didn't she?

Now she wondered if she'd allowed a single incident from the past to form her opinion. Nothing in Casey's current behavior spoke of deceit. He'd let her down, once, and had refused to give her details. And yet, she sensed there was more to the story. *Oh, Casey, why did you push me away? Why did I let you?*

"What was that?"

She startled at Reno's voice. "I…" Surely she hadn't spoken aloud? "I didn't say anything."

Eyebrows lifted, Reno rocked back on his heels. "You do realize he still has a thing for you."

She pretended ignorance. "*Who* still has a thing for me?"

"The man you can't stop watching."

*Oops.* "I'm watching my son."

"Sure, Sutton, let's go with that."

She closed her eyes and gave a slight sigh. Reno was fishing. He had to be. The best approach would be to evade and deflect. "Have you worked out what you're going to say when I hand you the microphone?"

His laugh came quick and easy. "Changing the subject, are we?"

"You better believe it. So…?"

"I have a few things planned. How much time before we take the stage?"

She checked the clock tower at the edge of the square. "A little under thirty minutes."

"Excellent." His gaze searched the crowd, landing on something—someone?—in the distance. He smiled, though a certain wariness had come into his eyes. "I'll be back in twenty."

"Make that fifteen."

"Yeah, sure. Okay." Without another word, he took off for parts unknown, his long legs eating up the ground at record speed.

"Don't be late, Reno," she called after his retreating back. Tonight was too important for Thunder Ridge's resident celebrity to flake out on her. "I'm serious. Do *not* be late or else."

He acknowledged the vague warning with a wave over his shoulder.

Shaking her head, Sutton checked the clock again. There was just enough time to make a fast circuit of the plaza. Hundreds of people occupied the area; just as many spilled down the sidewalks. Most were laughing, hugging one another, shouting out greetings, their voices raised loud enough to be heard above the Christmas music blaring from the outdoor speakers strategically placed along the square.

The noise was deafening, loud enough that parents had put noise-canceling headphones on their babies and young children. Yet, unlike at Quinn's house last weekend, Sutton's heart filled with joy.

No red flags, no awkward journey in her mind to her unhappy past. Tonight was business. Nothing personal. She knew the contradiction in her character would baffle most people. It did her. A psychologist would have a field day rummaging around in her mind.

Actually, one had, not long after Jeremy's death. The woman told Sutton it was common for people like her to have absolute control over one portion of their life and feel helpless in another.

And this wasn't the time for inner reflection. She was on duty. She'd worked hard planning tonight's events. Setting her mind solely on work, she surveyed the spoils of her efforts. Her decision to resist putting restrictions on the decorations had been a good one. The kaleidoscope of colors and themes blended well. An added touch of holiday cheer came from the residents themselves. Many had dressed themselves in traditional Christmas colors. Others had gone all out for the Ugly Christmas Sweater Contest that would be held later in the evening.

Smiling, she turned in a slow circle.

Thunder Ridge was ready. *She* was ready.

Where was Reno?

He'd already passed the ten-minute mark. She went in search of him. She ran into Quinn instead. Or rather, made eye contact with the woman from behind the impressive line at her hot chocolate bar. She gave Quinn a wave. The other woman waved back, then gestured her around to the back of the booth.

"Take this." Quinn handed her a to-go cup of steaming liquid. "You look like you could use it."

"I never turn down hot chocolate, especially yours." Sutton took a sip. "Wow, this is amazing."

Quinn beamed at the compliment. "Thanks. Now, let's blow our competitors away and win this contest. You with me, Mayor Wentworth?"

Hot with the thrill of competition, Sutton bumped fists with Quinn. "Let's do this."

Her phone dinged a five-minute warning. She looked up and grinned. "Showtime."

Sutton hurried to the stage, scanning the crowd as she went. Somewhere among the dense thicket of humanity were the magazine judges undercover as regular citizens. Her son was also out there with Casey.

But where was Reno?

She spotted him standing next to the Christmas tree, his eyes narrowed, his attention on the woman beside him. Silent and contemplative, Phoebe held Reno's stare, her face full of conflicting emotions. Her friend didn't notice Sutton's approach. Nor did Reno. She cleared her throat. When neither acknowledged her, she shouldered in between them. "I'm not interrupting anything, am I?"

Of course, she was, but neither said so. They were still staring—or rather, glaring—at each other.

"Anyway…" Sutton cleared her throat again. "Thank you, Phoebe, for setting up the life-size nutcrackers in place of barriers. It was a great solution for our traffic flow problem."

"Glad I could help."

Feeling as uncomfortable as the other two looked, Sutton cleared her throat a third time. And, really, that was quite enough of that. "It's time to get started, Reno. Ready to flip the switch?"

He gave her a cocky grin. "I was born ready."

Phoebe rolled her eyes, which Reno ignored in favor of moving toward the stage. He didn't bother saying goodbye to Phoebe. Not that the deputy noticed his rudeness. She was already walking away, shaking her head in obvious annoyance.

With time running out, Sutton mounted the stage ahead of Reno. He joined her and together they took their places behind the microphone. They'd already agreed that Sutton would kick things off. She opened her mouth to speak, then slammed it shut, aghast at what she saw. Right there, directly in her line of vision, was the six-foot plastic Santa dressed up like a Christmas caroler from the Victorian era.

Surely the contest judges spotted him, too. How could they not? There he stood, all by himself, looking absolutely ridiculous in a top hat, bright green scarf and flowing black cape. Would the judges see the humor in Casey's prank, or think the citizens of Thunder Ridge weren't taking the competition seriously?

"What's wrong, Sutton?" Reno asked.

"Give me a second." Turning her back to the crowd, she whipped out her phone and sent Casey a text. Not funny. Remove Santa, now.

No way. He wants to watch the show.

Typical Casey response. Okay, fine. He wanted to be difficult? She would simply circumvent him. She sent her next text to her assistant with very specific instructions. Almost immediately, the young woman appeared in the crowd, moving quickly, eyes locked on Santa.

Once Maria had hands on the decoration, Sutton stepped up to the microphone. "Merry Christmas, Thunder Ridge! Welcome to our annual tree-lighting ceremony."

Applause broke out.

Sutton continued her speech, her gaze sweeping over smiling faces, looking for two in particular. She found them near the back of the square. She was supposed to be irritated with Casey. She couldn't find it in her, not while Toby sat atop his shoulders, looking excited and waving frantically at her. Sutton's heart swooped in her chest when she saw her father was lined up beside Casey, smiling broadly, his hand hovering behind Toby's back as if ready to catch the boy if he toppled. She desperately wanted to join the three.

She wanted to step off the stage and...

The guilt came fast and hard. She should be thinking about Jeremy. And she was. But as the childhood friend he'd been, not the man she'd married. Tonight seemed to be bringing back all the wrong memories. Her guilt turned to grief and her words faltered.

*Keep it together*, she ordered herself. *Smile*.

She couldn't seem to pull off more than a shaky lift of her lips. Then she glanced at Casey. He gave her a thumbs-up and that's all it took. Her nerves settled.

Her voice steadied.

"And now," she said. "I'd like to introduce this year's Lighter of the Tree."

Hoots and hollers filled the cold night air.

"Many of you know him as one of our own, the downhill skier who became an international superstar. He's won world titles and too many gold medals to count. Some journalists have called him a national treasure. So, without further ado, I give you, Thunder Ridge's very own... Reno Miller."

As Sutton predicted, the applause was thunderous. "Reno, would you do us the honor of lighting our Christmas tree?"

"I'd be delighted." He made a grand show of placing his fingers on the external switch. "And… away…we… GO!"

A flick of his wrist and the Christmas tree came alive with thousands of twinkling lights. The effect was spectacular, as evidenced by the exclamations of awe and wonder. Then came the cheers. It was a glimmering keepsake of a moment. Sutton couldn't have asked for a more dramatic kickoff to the town's Christmas season.

Her eyes immediately went to her son. Toby was still on Casey's shoulders, clapping and cheering with the rest of Thunder Ridge. Casey kept his hands on the excited boy's legs, holding him steady, keeping him safe.

Gaze locked with hers, he tilted his head and gave her his signature smile, the one that could charm quills off a porcupine. Past folded over present. Sutton and Casey were teenagers again, attending the tree-lighting ceremony, holding hands, stealing away to sneak kisses under the mistletoe in the Gazebo. This time, when the memories came, there was no guilt. No remorse. Only a deep fondness. Warmth spread through every part of her being.

As if waking from a dream, Sutton put a hand to her forehead, pushed back her hair.

Slowly she became aware of her surroundings. Reno was still speaking, inviting the revelers to stick around for the Christmas Market and Ugly Christmas Sweater Contest. Eventually, he stepped back and motioned for her to take his place at the microphone.

"Thank you, Reno. How 'bout it, Thunder Ridge? Let's give it up for this year's Lighter of the Tree!"

Casey helped Toby off his shoulders. The boy bounced over to his grandfather as soon as his feet hit the ground. "Wasn't that cool, Grandpa?"

"Best part of my day."

Toby nodded enthusiastically. "Mine, too."

The older man glanced at Casey. "I appreciate you letting me know you were here. Thanks for calling me over."

The gratitude on the older man's face teased memories to the surface, memories from a time when Beau would have chosen a bottle of Scotch over spending the evening with his family. But that was in the past. What mattered was that he was here now, enjoying his grandson. "It wouldn't have been the same without you."

"It's been fun, but I need to get back. See you later, Toby."

Toby's face fell into a frown. "You're not sticking around, Grandpa?"

"Can't. I'm helping out at the face painting booth." He ruffled the boy's hair. "Stop by later and I'll paint you up good."

A quick, happy grin spread across the boy's face. "Can you do a superhero mask? Or maybe a pirate?"

Beau chuckled. "Whichever one you want."

"Cool."

The older man said goodbye, then disappeared into the crowd. With Toby looking up at him expectantly, Casey asked, "Want your face painted now, or should we go find your mother?"

"Mom! I think she'll want her face painted, too."

Not wanting to disagree, Casey made a noncommittal sound in his throat. The teenage Sutton would have been on board. The grown-up version? No way. Mayor Wentworth was too uptight. And he had a series of text messages concerning a plastic Santa to prove it.

"Where do you think Mom is?"

"Probably near the Christmas tree." She'd only just left the stage a few minutes ago. "Let's see if I'm right."

"Okay."

As they pushed through the crowd, Casey placed his hand on the boy's shoulder. He didn't want to lose Toby among the people meandering through the Christmas Market. The city council had offered him the opportunity to set up a temporary coffee shop. He'd given the idea a hard pass. Now he was glad he'd said no. Manning a booth meant he wouldn't have been able to spend the evening with Toby and Sutton, once they found her.

The smell of cinnamon and spiced apples mingled with cotton candy. Casey savored the greasy carnival-food scent. Toby seemed less impressed. The boy dragged his feet. His always-eager expression suddenly scrunched in a frown.

Casey exhaled sharply, recognizing the emotion behind the dejected body language and sad expression. He'd seen the same look in his mirror after receiving news of Jeremy's death. Sorrow, pain, bone-deep grief. Casey had lost a friend. But this boy had lost his dad. He wanted to pull the kid close and tell him everything was going to be all right. But that would be a lie. Toby's father was never coming home.

Pulling the boy to a halt, Casey swung around and bent down so he could look Toby in the eye. "What's wrong, little man?"

He glanced up, his watery eyes glistening under the streetlights. "I want to get my mom a Christmas present, but I don't know how." He whispered the words so softly Casey had to lean in close to hear. "My dad always took me shopping whenever he was home. Now—" he shrugged "—I'm not sure what to do."

The air around the boy crackled with distress. He looked so devastated Casey felt a tear push into his own eyes. There was a simple solution, of course. Toby had a grandfather. Beau would be more than willing to do his part. And yet, much like the situation with the soapbox car, Casey wanted to be the one to help the boy. *Don't do it*, he told himself. *Don't overstep.*

Ignoring his own advice, he made a spontaneous offer. "I'll take you shopping."

"For real?"

"For real." Except, now that reality was starting to set in, he felt a trickle of sweat sliding down his spine at the prospect of traipsing from store to store. He didn't hate shopping, precisely, so long as he had a list. Besides, Toby had a problem and Casey was in a position to solve it. He was doing this for the boy. That was what he told himself.

He almost believed it.

"Can we go now? Like right now?"

Casey went still for a heartbeat. The excited glint in the boy's eyes was all Jeremy. This was his friend's son, not his. Sorrow nearly buckled his knees. Casey would always be a poor substitute for the man they'd both lost. Yet, he wanted to try. The punch to his gut left him reeling and wondering how he'd managed to get himself in this deep, this fast, this completely.

"We'll go one day later this week," he croaked. "Maybe Tuesday. Or Wednesday. After we work on your car."

"I guess that would be okay."

Panic tried to take root. Casey refused to let it. His offer to take the kid shopping wasn't a big deal. He helped people all the time. Just the other day he'd played a role in saving the life of an accident victim by delivering several pints of blood. This wasn't much different.

Another trickle of sweat slid down his back. Fortunately, his cell phone vibrated with an incoming text. He checked the screen, let out a slow breath of relief. "My sister and Samson are looking for us." He stuffed the phone back in his pocket. "We're supposed to meet them at Quinn's booth."

They were nearly there when someone called out. "Toby!" Samson shouted again, waving frantically. "Toby! Over here. We're over here!"

Still waving, the little boy turned to Remy. She responded with a smile and a nod. And then he was running in their direction. He'd barely covered the distance when Toby asked, "Did you bring Roscoe with you?"

Roscoe was Samson's bulldog puppy from Clementine's previous litter. "No. I had to leave him at home, but if I'm good tonight he can sleep in my bed with me."

Pure little-boy envy filled Toby's eyes. "Lucky."

"I know!"

They fell into a discussion of what was better, sleeping with a puppy or sledding.

Remy, pushing a double stroller with two bundled-up children, eyed Casey with a speculative look. "Well, well. If it isn't Mr. Ebenezer Grinch himself gracing us with his presence."

"Hilarious."

"No. Really, all kidding aside, I didn't expect to see you tonight when you specifically said you weren't coming."

He shrugged. "I changed my mind."

"Right, because you've changed your mind approximately...never." Her eyebrows knit in a thoughtful frown. "Something's going on with you."

Nothing he wanted to share with his nosy little sister. "Maybe I'm a man of mystery, full of surprises. I zig when others zag."

"No, that would be me. You, on the other hand, are perfectly predictable. Until now. Which makes me wonder..." She glanced at Toby, then over to Sutton, who was currently heading in their direction. Though she still had a lot of ground to cover.

That gave Casey more time to watch her, something he never tired of doing. One second became two. Then three. After that, he lost count.

"Yep," Remy said, laughing softly beside him. "I was right. You, big brother, are perfectly predicable."

He'd been called worse. "Go away, Remy."

"Already gone." She took Samson and the babies with her, leaving Toby to wait next to Casey while Sutton finished her approach.

The rest of the evening went by in a blur. They ate junk food, bought trinkets, and let Beau paint their faces. When Casey arrived home, he had three things on his mind. Sutton, Toby and what role they might play in his future. He had no ready answers, only wishes and possibilities and a promise to himself he wouldn't mess things up with Sutton again.

The details, he decided, would sort themselves out in time.

# Chapter Eight

The following afternoon, Sutton drove out to Casey's house with her head full of details that still needed working out for Thunder Ridge's next big Christmas event. Because she had several meetings scheduled regarding the Torchlight Parade, Casey had offered to pick up Toby from school. Proving he had rotten timing, he'd sent a text at precisely 3:37 pm that read: The chicken is in the coop. I repeat, the chicken is in the coop.

Of course, the message had come through at a tense moment in her meeting with the fire chief and Sutton had been forced to swallow down her laughter. Now, as she turned onto Casey's property, she gave in to it. A half second later, she was growling in annoyance.

She slammed on the brakes and was out of her car in the next heartbeat. Hands on hips, mouth gaping open, she stared at Casey's house for a solid thirty seconds. He'd put up one—just one—anemic strand of lights that had large gaping holes where several of the bulbs had burned out. Had he bothered to add a cheery wreath to the front door, or garland to the easements, or a silver bell—anywhere? Well, no, of course not.

Excited chatter and rock music filled the late-afternoon air. Sutton easily picked out her son's voice. Her uncle's. Casey's. And then, her father's booming laughter rose above it all. It was the sound of her childhood. She braced for the black cloud to descend over her. Nothing happened. She moved a step closer and waited for her sense of time and place to tangle together in her mind. Again, nothing.

Huh. Was she actually on the road to recovery from the trauma of her childhood?

She listened a little longer. There was happiness in that garage, lots of happiness. And Casey was the reason. He'd gathered the men of her family together in support of her son. The man was proving to be more than he seemed on the surface, and everything she remembered from their childhood. Kind, loyal, thoughtful…

Oh, no. Sutton wasn't falling for him again. It helped to look at the gorgeous house and his pitiful attempt at decorating it for Christmas. She retrieved her phone and kept her text brief. Meet me outside your house.

Be right there.

Casey soon appeared beside her. Unlike Sutton, who wore her heaviest coat and thick snow boots, he wasn't dressed for the weather. The cold temperatures didn't seem to bother him. She found that oddly endearing. Or maybe it was the way his entire demeanor exuded strength and reliability. She tried to swallow, but the muscles in her throat wouldn't cooperate.

His eyebrows shot up. "You texted?"

There was just enough snark in his tone to goad her into stabbing a finger in the general vicinity of his house. "That," she fumed, never once taking her eyes off his face. "*That's* how you decorate? With one pitiful string of lights?"

"I actually put up two."

"One. Two. Whatever. You're missing the point, Casey."

"No, Sutton, *you're* missing the point." His expression never changed, but she could feel a coldness creeping into their conversation that had nothing to do with the frigid temperatures swirling around them. "You told me to decorate my house, or rather demanded it, and so I did. End of discussion."

"Really, Casey? You know I meant for you to put up more than one strand of lights."

"I've done what you asked," he said, his tone flat, his pale blue eyes as brittle as ice. "And now I'm going to ask you to leave it alone."

"You know I can't do that."

Silence, hard and distancing, fell between them.

Something wasn't right here. Sutton sensed Casey pulling away from her. A coiled, barely contained moodiness rolled off him. "Casey, please. Help me understand why you're so resistant to decorating your house."

"Let it alone, Sutton. I'm asking you as a friend."

She glanced toward the string of lights, back to him. "What happened to you, Casey?"

Or was it a who? A *she*? Sutton hadn't let her mind go there before, but now she did. Was a woman to blame for Casey's change of heart?

"Casey." This time, she did reach to him and touched his arm. He didn't flinch away, a good sign, one that gave her the courage to slide her hand down his forearm and clasp her fingers around his. "Talk to me."

He said nothing, his expression no longer cold but ice-cold, completely shutting her out. She'd seen that look before, the day after his arrest, and the two weeks that followed. The distance he put between them hurt just as much today as it had all those years ago.

Her heartbeat surged at the pain she saw, raw and vulnerable, in his hollow gaze. She recognized the emptiness in him and the desire to walk away from her. Not again. She had to get through to him. But how?

She squeezed his hand. It was the wrong thing to do. He pulled free of her grip,

"Something happened to you. No, don't deny it. If you would tell me what it was, perhaps I could—"

She was talking to his retreating back. And wow, the man could really move when he put his mind to it. Trotting after him, she entered the garage a full ten steps behind. Her son's laughter hit her first, followed by her father's raspy voice. She paused on the threshold, drew in a breath. The smell of freshly sawed wood mingled with motor oil.

It was an oddly pleasant scent that brought back equally pleasant memories. She battled them back and watched Casey move in beside Toby. He leaned over the boy and guided his hand that held a wrench. Once Toby had the technique down, Casey stood back.

Toby's brow furrowed in concentration and he caught his tongue between his teeth as he worked the wrench the way Casey showed him. Toby said something to Casey over his shoulder, but Sutton couldn't hear her son's words over the music. She thought he might have asked, "Is this right?"

Casey quietly studied the boy's technique before reaching down and guiding his hand again. A flash of memory hit Sutton so hard the impact shoved her back a step. She was standing in another garage, and Casey was working on another car.

The two of them had leaned over the engine while he showed her how to use a socket wrench, his hand over hers, guiding her through the process, their earlier laughter gone.

Next thing she remembered the tool was on the garage floor and they were in each other's arms. She shook her head, forcing her mind back to the present. Casey wasn't that boy anymore, and she wasn't that girl. Sutton must, must, *must* remember that.

They'd had their chance. There were no do-overs in life. Jeremy's death had taught her that. Needing a distraction from her own miserable thoughts, she wandered over to Clementine's basket. Winston had wedged himself in beside her, as had the two remaining puppies. The sight of the contented foursome sleeping soundlessly was a shot to the heart.

There'd been no family snuggles with Jeremy after Toby's birth. Her husband had been deployed when their son made his entrance into the world. In fact, he'd missed the first six months of Toby's life.

Sighing, Sutton sat on the floor and watched

the dogs slumber. One of the puppies cracked open an eye, saw her, then proceeded to wiggle out from his spot between Winston and Clementine. She went palms up in the universal show of surrender. "Oh no. No way. I am not picking you up."

He continued toward her, snorting and huffing, rolling over, standing up, face-planting, and then doing it all again. By the time he managed to waddle over to her, she was smitten. And now, she was holding the puppy, cooing to him, raining kisses on his neck, his head, whispering nonsensical words that may have included a promise of undying love.

"You know you want to take him home with you." The voice belonged to her dad.

"Not even a little bit."

"What was that?" he asked, cupping a hand over his ear as he joined her on the floor. "I didn't quite catch what you said with your face buried in Louie's neck and all."

She glanced up. "Louie?"

"The puppy." Beau jerked his chin at the animal. "Casey let Toby name him."

"Oh, he did, did he?" She was going to have to explain to Casey, again, for the millionth time, that he was not to overstep where her son was concerned. Allowing Toby to name a puppy was definitely overstepping.

Her father ruffled Louie's fur. "Cute little guy, isn't he?"

"Adorable. But no, Dad. Louie is not coming home with Toby and me, not today, tomorrow, or on Christmas Day. And you are not getting involved. Understand?"

"I understand."

"Good." Sutton set the animal back in the basket.

There. She was done playing with puppies. One problem. Louie wasn't done with her. He whined. Wiggled his bottom. Then made a heroic leap. Sutton caught him midair and dangled him in front of her face so that they were eye to eye. Louie panted happily, looking thrilled and totally on board for whatever this new game was. She would not pull him close. She would not.

"Hey, Mom, Louie likes you."

"He's a puppy," she said without inflection. "He likes everyone."

"Yeah," Toby agreed. "But he really, really likes you. And me. Especially me. Can I hold him?"

She eyed the animal straining in her hands, his little legs running in the air as he tried to get to her. Before she fell deeper in love, she kissed his head, then passed him to her son. "Here you go."

Her eyes filled with tears as she took in her very happy son sitting beside his grandfather while they both played with the puppy. The other baby bulldog began belly-crawling to the edge of the basket. He wiggled over the top and tumbled onto the floor. Sutton couldn't help herself. She scooped up the little fur ball. She considered kissing the adorable face, but the puppy beat her to it, getting in several licks across her chin.

Laughing over the impromptu bath, she stood and studied the animal through narrowed eyes. A second later, she gave in to temptation and pressed her lips to the furry head. "You are seriously cute."

"He's available for adoption," Casey said, coming up beside her, his eyes clear of the storm clouds she'd seen in them earlier. "With an immediate delivery date."

With considerable reluctance, she handed him the animal. "I'm sure you'll find him an exceptional home."

"Why would I do that? When we both know it's only a matter of time before you cave into your son's pleas and take one of the little guys home with you."

"Not a chance," she said, reaching for the puppy again, stopping herself just in time. But oh, my. She really, really wanted to hold him again. The desire was strong. She closed her eyes and tried to ride it out.

"Go on, Sutton," Casey urged in a low, husky whisper. "Take him."

She opened her eyes. "Oh, all right. Hand him over."

Bulldog exchange complete, Casey breathed in deep, drawing in Sutton's floral scent. The puppy obscured her face, but not enough that he couldn't see the pleasure written across her features. Her beauty struck him hard. He forced a smile to hide the ache in his throat. He liked Sutton, always had, always would. No other woman engaged his mind and sparked his humor like she did, not even Victoria.

Casey had told himself it didn't matter. But his ex-fiancée had sensed he wasn't all in. She'd been right to break things off. Why had it taken him this long to see that? Because Sutton hadn't been in his life like she was now. Every hour he spent with her made him want more. She captivated him, filled him with hope, made him want to be a better man. Yeah, Victoria had been right to call things off.

Sighing softly, Sutton shifted the puppy in her hands. The move gave him a better view of her face. Gone was the I'm-in-charge mayoral glower. In its place was the tender expression she usually reserved for Toby. Casey liked being on the receiving end of that look.

Time seemed to bend and shift, calling to him to take a chance. Then she took a deep breath and buried her face in puppy fur again. A lump formed in his throat as he watched her lavish the animal with unbridled affection. He wanted to go to Sutton and pull her into his arms. She'd stolen his heart when they were kids and had never given it back.

Casey had been seven at the time, Sutton six months older. She'd been transferred into his second grade class and had been assigned the desk next to his. He'd greeted her with a grin and an offer to show her how to play foursquare at recess. It was the start, as they say, of a beautiful friendship. By senior year, they were deeply in love. Promises were made. The future was discussed. And then, one fateful night, Casey's decision to protect Jeremy, and Sutton was lost to him forever.

Desperate to lighten the mood, he said, "You're slobbering all over my dog."

She lifted her head. With the faintest trace of amusement shadowing her mouth, she skimmed her gaze over the puppy's fur. "Oops."

And then she laughed.

Casey's heart stuttered at the sound. Laughter suited her. Her face glowed with happiness. He was pretty sure his did, too, because he felt heat building beneath his skin.

Whoa. He needed to slow things down. He needed to think. Calmly. His mind was going too fast, or maybe not fast enough. Sutton was becoming too important to him, as was her son.

"Casey?" Sutton placed a hand on his arm, bringing him back to the moment. To her. "Toby told me you're taking him Christmas shopping. It was nice of you to offer, seriously, but it's not necessary. I can take him myself, I don't mind. Actually, I want to."

"He asked me for a reason."

"I'm sure he did, but like I said, it's not necessary."

Casey watched her closely, looking for something in her face, not sure what he hoped to find. "You got a problem with me spending time with Toby?"

"Not at all."

Her answer came too fast. "You don't trust me with him?"

"I trust you. Of course I do." Her voice was far away now, her gaze drifting over his shoulder to latch onto her son. "It's just, you're already sacrificing a lot of time away from your businesses to help him build his car for the derby."

Casey let the insult roll off. "It's not a sacrifice."

"Right. Sorry. Poor choice of words." Sighing,

she set the puppy on the floor. "It's just… I don't understand why he asked you instead of me."

Ah, now they were getting somewhere. It wasn't that Toby asked Casey to take him shopping, it was that he hadn't asked his mom. "Think about it, Sutton. Why would your kid ask me to take him Christmas shopping instead of you?"

"I don't know, I— Oh." She lifted her hands, let them flutter to her sides. "*Oh*. He wants to buy me a gift?"

He tapped her on the nose. "Bingo."

"But…" She swept her gaze through the garage, stopping on Beau. "My father can take him."

"I already offered. Toby and I have it all planned. Come on, Sutton. Let me do this for him. Let me do it for you."

"Oh, Casey. I…okay." She gave him a watery smile. "Thank you."

"You're welcome."

Surprising himself, her—both of them—he pulled her close, planted a fast kiss on her mouth, then stepped back.

As kids, Casey had considered Sutton his best friend. As teenagers, he'd considered her the love of his life. As adults, now, in this moment, after a practically nonexistent kiss, the emotion spreading through him felt like forever.

Sutton seemed to be waiting for him to say something. To *do* something. Casey didn't know what to say, what to do. Kiss her again? Pretend it never happened? He felt a cold wave roll through him, squeezing the pit of his stomach. He barely said goodbye before calling out to Toby. "Break's over, little man. Let's get back to work."

## Chapter Nine

Early Sunday morning, while Sutton washed the breakfast dishes, she allowed her mind to wander back to the previous afternoon in Casey's garage. Until now, she'd avoided thinking about their encounter and the way he'd kissed her. What had possessed him to do such a thing? And why had she been tempted to kiss him back, right there in front of her son, her father, her uncle, and four adorable bulldogs?

She was still thinking about it when Toby bulleted past her in a flash of little-boy urgency. "Hurry up, Mom," he shouted over his shoulder. "Let's get going already."

"What's the rush?" Usually Sutton was the one pushing her son to get moving on Sunday morning.

He paused at the door leading into the garage, impatience making him bounce on his toes. "Because Miss Summerland made us all promise we wouldn't be late for the play, especially those of us with speaking parts."

Ah, of course. It was a big day for her son. No wonder he was excited. Toby had been cast as the lead shepherd boy in the children's Christmas pageant at the local high school. But the curtain wasn't scheduled to rise for several hours yet, and not until after Sunday morning service, which was still thirty minutes away. "We have plenty of time, Toby."

No sooner had she said this than the boy disappeared into the garage. Two seconds later, he popped his head back into the house. "Come. On. *Mom!*"

Sutton wasn't sure whether to be amused or exasperated by her son's bossiness. Keeping her voice even, she said, "Watch your tone, kiddo."

He hung his head. "Sorry."

"I know you are, baby."

"So…" He lifted his chin and cast a smile in her direction. "Can we go now?"

"We can go now."

As they piled into her car, Sutton let her own excitement bubble to the surface. The children's Christmas pageant should give Thunder Ridge an advantage in the contest over their fiercest competitor. Village Green wasn't putting on anything remotely similar to the family-friendly production. In fact, they didn't have anything planned for Sunday afternoon. Feeling smug, she backed out into the street, put the car in gear, and eyed the dark wall of clouds blowing in from the west.

A snowstorm brewed in the distance, promising the ten inches of fresh powder the local weatherman predicted. An excellent turn, as far as Sutton was concerned. The additional snow would add a lovely ambience to the upcoming Christmas events, especially the Torchlight Parade.

"I wonder if Mr. Casey will be at church this morning?"

Sutton wondered the same thing. But where her son was excited over the prospect, she had several concerns. Would yesterday's kiss make things awkward between them? Or would they both pretend nothing had happened? Since that was how they'd handled the decorating situation yesterday, she figured they would continue in that vein. Assuming Casey attended morning service. It was a busy time of year for him.

She found a parking space in the church's lot and looked around. Casey's vintage truck was nowhere in sight, nor was either of his muscle cars. Disappointed, she cut the engine.

"Hey, Mom, look! Mr. Casey's already here. See? He's standing on the church steps."

Oh, boy, was he ever. Sutton could only stare at the picture he made dressed in jeans and a tan sweater beneath his leather bomber jacket. With the snow-covered mountains as his backdrop, the man looked larger than life. But then he smiled, and there was the boy she'd once loved with all her heart.

"Mr. Casey," Toby shouted the moment he was out of the car. "Mr. Casey, over here!"

Hand in the air, he started down the steps.

Toby ran to meet him. Sutton made the trek at a much slower pace, mesmerized by the way Casey bent down to listen to something her son said. He paid close attention, as if everything Toby said was of the utmost importance. In that moment, he was more of a father than Jeremy had ever been.

The thought was an uncharitable one. And Sutton was ashamed of herself. It wasn't Jeremy's fault he'd been deployed most of Toby's childhood. He'd been an excellent father when he was home and not distracted with preparations for his next mission. And that was also uncharitable. Jeremy's dedication to his job had been one of the things she'd loved most about him.

Still, it was nice to see Toby receiving consistent male attention, not only from her father and uncle, but now from Casey, as well. Sutton wasn't supposed to feel this sense of gratitude. She wasn't supposed to feel appreciation for a man who'd let her down so completely once before. *When you were kids.*

The thought pulled her up short. Was she being petty? Holding on to a hurt that had happened over a decade ago? Not a hurt, she reminded herself, a betrayal.

So why did Casey still tug at hidden places in her heart no one had ever touched except him. Another traitorous thought that Sutton shoved aside with all the others. Casey was only in their lives temporarily. In a few short weeks, they would go their separate ways and that would be that.

Her father called out to her. She responded with what she hoped was a smile that reflected how pleased she was to see him. Because she was pleased. "Morning, Dad."

"Morning." He pulled her into a hug.

Surprising herself, she leaned into the embrace before letting him go. "Will you be sitting with Toby and me?"

"Try and stop me."

They laughed in unison, then made their way toward the church side by side. Casey looked up from his conversation with Toby. When their eyes met, Sutton felt the same nervous excitement she'd experienced when they were teenagers. "Hi," she said on a rush of air.

"Hi." An awkward moment passed, then he tipped his head toward her father. "Beau, always good to see you."

"Always good to see you, too, Casey."

Toby tugged on Sutton's sleeve. "We're all sitting together, right?"

"Are we?" she asked Casey.

"Of course we are."

With Casey and Toby leading the way, they found seats in one of the back pews of the church. Almost immediately, the worship band took its place. Of course, Casey had a boy band voice. Sutton gave a little shake of her head. How fair was that? Two songs later, the youth pastor called the children forward. With only the briefest of farewells, Toby scrambled out of the pew and hustled to the front of the church with all the other kids.

Sitting on the steps leading up to the altar, the pastor gave a short sermon about the parable of the lost sheep and how much God loves all His children. He concluded with a question. "Who's ready for the Christmas pageant?"

All hands shot up.

"Then we better go rehearse." As he escorted the children out of the church, the senior pastor took his place at the pulpit.

Although he'd been a freshman her senior year, and they'd rarely interacted, Sutton remembered Brandon Stillwell from high school. He'd been completely undisciplined, more than a little wild, and a total risk-taker. He wasn't supposed to amount to anything, that was what the town gossips said, what *everyone* said. The year he spent in jail brought hard evidence to their claims.

But Brandon had changed. He'd calmed down, gone to seminary, and was a powerful preacher of the Word. He had a build like an NFL linebacker, sandy-brown hair, pale amber eyes, and a penetrating stare he used to compel the congregation into silence.

He gave the opening prayer, then launched into his sermon with a personal story from his days as a juvenile delinquent. He had everyone laughing and nodding. "It would be easy for me to claim the trouble I got into wasn't my fault. So what if my buddies and I raced down the mountain highway at a hundred miles an hour without our headlights on. It was midnight. The roads were empty. We were just having fun. We didn't hurt anyone. No harm, no foul."

More nodding, a few shocked gasps, a pair of groans from his former compatriots.

"I could blame my behavior on the company I kept." He made eye contact with Reno, then Wyatt, both of whom were right there with him during that insane flight down the mountain. And most of the other shenanigans. "But that would be both wrong and inaccurate. Every decision I made, good, bad or reckless, was mine and mine alone."

He paused, letting those words sink in.

"God forgave me, no question, and, yeah, I pulled that night off. But more reckless acts followed. My bad choices led to even worse habits that took years to break."

Compelled by some inner nudging, Sutton looked over at her father. His bad choices had also led to bad habits. But, like Brandon, he'd changed his ways by making different choices. It couldn't have been easy and was probably still a daily battle.

Humbled by his courage, she covered her father's hand and squeezed gently. A moment of understanding passed between them, followed by a wave of peace she hadn't felt in her father's company—ever. *This is what forgiveness feels like.*

"So what does any of this story have to do with Christmas?" Brandon asked. "A lot, actually. Let's turn to Matthew, chapter one." He read verses eighteen and nineteen aloud, then looked up again. "This portion of the narrative depicts the choices, actions and habits of a righteous man. Joseph was put in a difficult position. He could have abandoned Mary and, according to the mores of the day, would have been justified doing so. But his first concern was for the woman he'd pledged to marry, not himself."

Brandon paused, looked out over the congregation, then continued, "Joseph chose to put his own self-interest aside and act on another person's behalf. That decision changed everything for Mary, for her unborn child, for the world."

Sutton shifted in her seat, glanced down at her lap. Out of the corner of her eye, she saw Casey sit up straighter, his lips pressed tightly together.

"Joseph's single act reveals an undeniable truth. We aren't the only ones affected by our decisions. Often, our actions have unintended consequences."

Sutton knew all about unintended consequences. She tried again to capture Casey's eye, to see if there was guilt in them. What she saw was something else entirely. Grief. Sorrow. A silent plea for...what? What was he asking of her?

She lifted a questioning eyebrow. He glanced away, his disappointment clear.

A memory nagged at her. Casey had looked at her like that once before, the day after her birthday party. What had he said? Something about doing the wrong thing for a good reason. She'd never understood what he meant. Jeremy had been equally cryptic, although his words had been about loyalty and friendship. Something about Casey being a better person than he was. What had Jeremy meant? Had Casey—

No. She pushed the thought out of her mind, because with it came the sharp feeling of betrayal. Not from Casey, or from Jeremy, but from them both. Had she been so caught up in her own misery that she'd fail to comprehend the reason behind Casey's lack of remorse and Jeremy's unwavering loyalty to his friend? Sutton thought about her husband's dedication to his job, so strong, nearly fanatical, as if he were making up for some past wrong. And—

No, it was too terrible to contemplate. How could she think so little of the man she'd married? She'd thought that little of Casey. And he'd let her. He'd let Sutton think the worst of him. So had, in his own way, Jeremy. Had both men lied to her? Only one of them could tell her the truth now. She glanced over at Casey.

He was slipping out of the pew, heading toward the door. She started to go after him, but Brandon's voice stopped her. "I leave you with this final thought. Trouble is a single, bad decision away, as evidenced by my own life. However, healing, forgiveness, a restored relationship is but a single good decision away. And that, my friends, leads to a greater reward."

He continued speaking, but Sutton wasn't listening anymore. She was too busy gazing at Casey's retreating back, wondering, worrying, praying for insight.

"Let us pray."

Sutton lowered her head, promising herself she would uncover the truth. With or without Casey's cooperation, she would know what really happened the night of her eighteenth birthday.

Casey couldn't get out of the church building fast enough. He pushed himself to move quickly, but not so quickly as to draw attention to himself. Too late. A quick glance over his shoulder told him Sutton was watching him with that shrewd, calculating look he'd seen in her eyes once before. Putting two and two together.

Was she coming up with four, or still not getting it?

Casey shrugged. Sutton could search for the truth. That was her right. But she'd get no help from him. He'd made a promise to his friend, and Jeremy had gone to his grave trusting Casey would keep his secret. He would honor that. No matter how hard Sutton pushed.

There was an easy solution, of course. Casey would simply keep his distance. Ditching the pageant was a good first step, except that would hurt Toby. Casey wouldn't hurt that kid. He couldn't. It wasn't in his nature. He would sit in the back of the auditorium. Far, far away from Sutton.

Casey Evans was his name. Avoidance was his game.

He was feeling pretty good about his plan, then Brandon's words echoed in his head. *We aren't the only ones affected by our decisions.* Casey's decision to protect Jeremy had harmed Sutton. He knew that now. Maybe he'd always known it, but he'd convinced himself she'd walked away a little too easily to be truly hurt. When she'd married Jeremy, Casey told himself she'd moved on. And so had he.

But had he, really?

Too much thinking. He had to get out of his head. What he needed was a distraction. Working the espresso machine would do the trick. His feet carried him faster down the sidewalk and straight into Cargo Coffee. He looked around. The shop was surprisingly busy, considering most church services hadn't let out yet. His manager, Emory, pinned him with her eyes and mouthed the word *Help!*

He dove right in.

Fifteen minutes later, he was in a groove. Emory called out the next order. "I need four skinny lattes, two caramel macchiatos and—" she consulted the computer printout in her hand "—a peppermint mocha, no whip."

Casey nodded, then got to work. While steaming milk for the lattes, he glanced idly about the shop, and that was when he saw him. Santa, in all his plastic glory, lined up with the regular paying customers waiting to give their order at the cash register.

Casey's smile came quick and his mood instantly lifted. Someone had not only inserted Santa into the line, but they'd dressed him in a red sweater with matching booties. And there, on the top of his head, was a pair of reindeer antlers exactly like the ones Casey had put on Winston.

"Take over for me," he told Emory. At her questioning stare, he pointed to Santa.

"Gotcha." Her accompanying laugh brought out his own.

As he circled around the counter, Casey swept his gaze over the interior of the coffee shop. Sutton was nowhere in sight. He hadn't actually expected to see her. She was too crafty to be caught that easily.

He might have fallen a little in love with her right then, if he was keeping track of such things. Which he most definitely was not. He zeroed in on Santa. If Casey wasn't mistaken, the old guy had moved several feet closer to the front counter.

Leaning in, he gave the ridiculous decoration the stink eye. Santa didn't react. What did he expect from a plastic yard ornament?

"Who's responsible for this guy?" He flapped his hand in Santa's direction. "And how much is the mayor paying you?"

Not a single person piped up. Nor did anyone actually look in his direction. Did Sutton have the entire town on her side? Possibly. Probably.

Might as well play along. He grabbed Santa by the shoulders. "All right, buddy, you're coming with me. You don't have any pockets, so I know you're not here to buy coffee."

Snickers followed him as he dragged the decoration into his office. Confident he was alone, he whipped out his phone and sent a one-word text to Sutton. Respect.

Her response was a smiley face emoji.

How'd you pull it off?

Floating bubbles showed up on his phone. A second later... You tell me your ways and I'll tell you mine.

He didn't have to think about his answer. No way. Not a chance.

More bubbles, then: Give it up, Evans. Admit defeat. Bow to the master.

His reply required less thought than the one before. No way. Not a chance.

Her next text had him shaking his head. By my calculations I'm up by several points. Want to call a truce?

He might be repeating himself, but why mess with perfection? So he responded: No way. Not a chance.

Me, neither.

And that, he decided, was why no other woman had been able to cut through his defenses and win his heart. Sutton had set the bar too high. She was so completely capable and clever and gorgeous it made his chest ache with a pressure that threatened to break him. Whatever conclusion Casey had come to about keeping his distance vanished. She'd won him over. Hook, line and a six-foot plastic Santa.

Speaking of Santa, Casey thought through his options, rubbed his jaw, checked his watch, then decided the old guy could wait. He returned to work, eyeing the door every time someone entered his shop. Not that he was looking for anyone in particular. No, no, not him.

Fifteen minutes prior to the start of the Christmas pageant, business slowed to nonexistent. Casey put Emory in charge of the shop, since that was what he paid her for, and entered the high school auditorium with five minutes to spare. Three rows from the front, Sutton sat with her father and uncle. And, well, well, well, she'd left an empty spot next to her on the aisle. A spot that Casey could fill without having to climb over half the population of Thunder Ridge.

He plopped down, stretched out his legs, and hit Sutton with the full force of his charm. "Thanks for saving me a seat."

Two perfectly arched eyebrows shot up. "Who said I was saving it for you?"

"Santa sang like a canary."

"Nope. Santa's my guy. He would never rat me out."

"Oh, he didn't give you up right away. I grilled him. He responded with snark. Things were implied. Insults were hurled. Matters got ugly for a while."

"Now, that," she said, lips twitching, "I can fully accept. I'm sure he—"

"Shh. I'm not finished."

She rolled her eyes. "By all means, continue."

"Where was I?"

"Insults, snark." She leaned in close, so close he could see the striations of blue on blue in her irises. And the smile she couldn't quite keep off her lips. "Any of that ringing a bell?"

"All of it." He tried not to notice how his heart beat against his ribs as though it wanted to take flight. Or how he really, really wanted to kiss those pretty smiling lips. "Anyway, it seems *your guy* is easily bribed."

She sat back. "How easily?"

"It took a plate of cookies, a glass of milk, and as you can see, ta-da—" Casey lifted his hands, palms up "—here I am, filling the seat you saved for me."

Sutton gave him a slow, measured clap. "Beautiful piece of fiction, Casey. Really. I laughed. I cried. I cringed."

He gave her a mock bow from the waist up. "You're welcome." He would have said more, but a series of chiming bells dinged over the loudspeaker. "We'll finish this conversation later."

Sutton crinkled her nose adorably. "Thank you, no. I'll pass."

"Suit yourself." They were both smiling when the lights dimmed.

They were still smiling when the curtain began to rise. A silent message passed between them before they broke eye contact and settled back in their chairs to watch the show. The moment Toby took the stage, Casey's hand found Sutton's. She held on tight, mouthing along with her son as he recited his lines.

That was when it clicked, when Casey realized he was in love with Sutton. Not with the girl she'd been, but the woman she was today. The devoted mother to an amazing little boy. The dedicated mayor who would put Thunder Ridge on every top-ten list known to man.

She was also the woman Casey had lied to for over a decade. There could be no future for them. Only the present, the right now. It was an unexpected gift he didn't deserve, one he wouldn't squander. He would shore up every happy memory he could with Sutton and Toby and tuck each one away in his heart.

Then, somehow, he would let them go.

But not yet.

For the next three weeks, Sutton and Toby were still his, all his.

# *Chapter Ten*

Even before the lights came up in the auditorium, Sutton noticed a change come over Casey. The color deepened in his face. His brow furrowed. The small muscles around his eyes and mouth contorted with some powerful emotions. She knew that expression, had seen it before when they were younger. He'd come to some sort of a conclusion that didn't sit well. "Are you all right?" she asked him.

"Sure." He produced a fleeting half smile. "Never better."

His face, brooding in the flickering shadows, told a different story. As they both got to their feet, he seemed...stricken. But then another change came over him and he looked straight into her eyes with a tenderness that she knew was reserved solely for her. That intense, sweet gaze burned through her composure. She felt the sudden sensation of falling. Lightly his fingers came to her arm, just above the elbow, a careful pressure that grounded her.

Her father spoke into the heavy silence that had descended between them. "Sutton, your uncle and I are going to head over to the Latte Da. We'll snag us a table for…" He leaned around her and addressed Casey directly, "Five?"

Without taking his eyes off Sutton, he nodded. "I could eat."

"Good. Excellent. We'll see you over there." A shuffle of feet followed as the two older men exited down the center aisle.

Sutton was left staring into Casey's eyes. Breathless and agitated, she couldn't find a thing to say. Casey seemed equally captured in the moment. They were having some sort of silent conversation with their eyes. If only Sutton understood what was being said she might be able to unstick her tongue from the roof of her mouth.

More staring ensued, broken by Toby. "Mom. Hey, Mom. *Mom*, did you see me? I got all my lines right."

Sutton lowered to the ground until her face was level with her son's. "You were simply amazing." Tenderly she smoothed a hand over his dark, ruffled hair. "Best lead shepherd boy in the entire play."

"Gee, Mom, whatever. I was the *only* lead shepherd boy."

"And still the best."

Grinning, Toby looked up at the tall man beside her with a flicker of uncertainty. "What did you think, Mr. Casey?"

"I think you gave a riveting, award-winning performance."

Toby's face went blank. "Huh?"

"You stole the show, little man. I've never been prouder." Casey snatched up the smiling boy and spun him in a small, tight circle before setting him back on his feet. "This calls for a celebration."

Toby considered this. "Can I have ice cream?"

"Yes," Casey and Sutton said in unison.

The boy bounced his gaze from one to the other. "Like, can we go get it now?"

"Yes," they said again, their voices actually harmonizing this time.

Toby laughed. "You two are so weird together."

Out of the mouths of babes, Sutton thought, deciding to take her son's proclamation as a compliment rather than an insult. By the sound of his chuckle, Casey must have come to the same conclusion.

Despite what they told Toby, it actually took them a full fifteen minutes to exit the high school. They spent most of that time speaking with Casey's siblings, all of whom either had a child in the play or, as in McCoy's case, was there to support his nieces and nephews.

After a brief debate, the three of them, plus her father and uncle, ended up sitting at a table with Casey's family, enjoying ice cream and conversation. Sutton realized with a jolt that this would have been her life if she and Casey had never broken up.

But they hadn't stayed together and Sutton wanted to know why. The more she reviewed the events of that night in her mind, the more she realized that the facts simply didn't add up. As a trial attorney she'd learned to look past the obvious. Or, as one of her law professors had drilled into her: *You will never win a trial on eyewitness accounts alone. People rarely remember every detail as it actually occurred. It's your job to find out what's hovering beneath the surface of their memories.*

Sage words and excellent advice she would apply to this situation. She heard her name, coming at her in Casey's voice. She turned her head and gave him a long look. "What?"

"Your ice cream is turning into soup."

"Oh…yikes. You're right." She picked up her spoon, scooped up a decidedly soupy bite.

"Where were you?" he asked. "I thought I lost you there for a minute."

"I was, uh… I was just thinking."

"About…?"

She glanced to her left, smiled. "Actually, I wasn't thinking, I was being *riveted* by Toby and Samson's argument over which of them is going to win their division in the derby."

"Riveted, huh?"

Pleased he'd hooked on the word, she felt her mouth curve. "It seems to be the word of the day, probably listed on one of those calendars people buy to expand their vocabulary."

This made him laugh. "Are you calling me out?"

Yeah, she was. Or she would be, once she finished digging into their shared past. Casey had no idea what was coming. It was only fair she warn him, in a vague sort of way. Picking up her spoon, Sutton pointed it in his direction. "I'm on to you, Casey Evans."

"Ohhhh, that sounds ominous." He gave a mock shudder. "Should I be afraid?"

She gave him a get-serious look, which he mimicked to perfection. "You should be very afraid, I—" She broke off with a laugh. "Is that really how I look when I scowl? All scrunched up like that?"

"Yeah, but on you it's adorable."

That, she decided, was the perfect place to end their discussion. The rest of the evening was filled with laughter and more joking. Sutton ate too much ice cream, but she couldn't find it in her to care about the extra calories. She'd had too much fun with Casey and their respective families.

The next morning, when she was sitting at her desk, dreaming of salted caramel ice cream and the way Casey's smile made her heart ping, a text came in from the man himself. Would you mind bringing Toby out to my house this afternoon?

Sutton thumbed back a quick reply. Sure. No problem. She thought about leaving it at that, knowing if Casey needed to switch things up this afternoon, he had a reason. Still, she asked him, Everything all right?

Nothing I can't handle.

Ho-kay, that wasn't cryptic at all. She thought about pressing for an explanation, but her office phone started ringing and she let it go. The day got away from her after that, partly because her phone continued ringing with important calls and partly because she fell down a rather large rabbit hole while researching Colorado state law pertaining to underage drinking. She was still surfing around when the alarm on her phone went off.

Time to pick up Toby from school.

Unfortunately, her phone rang yet again, requiring more than a brief response. She was stopped twice more on her way out the building, once by Marie and then by Carl, the city manager. So here she sat, at the back of the carpool line. The very back.

Sighing, she climbed out of her BMW and moved to stand on the sidewalk where Toby would see her. Sutton wasn't the only one enjoying the bright sunshine. Quinn stood three cars up beside an oversize SUV.

Sutton waved. The other woman waved back. Then made the short trek over. "Fun times last night at the Latte Da."

Sutton nodded. "Very fun. Toby couldn't stop talking about it when we got home."

"Same with the girls." Quinn squeezed her arm. "I'm glad you and the rest of your family joined us."

"Me, too."

They shared a smile. A real one. And maybe, just maybe, they were on the road to restoring their friendship. There were a few remaining obstacles, but Sutton was hopeful.

"I need to say this," Quinn began, looking slightly uncomfortable. "So let me say it, okay?"

Sutton stared into the woman's warm, troubled eyes, then nodded solemnly. "Okay."

"What you're doing for Thunder Ridge, all the added touches to the Christmas events, reinstating the Soap Box Derby, the contest itself. It's really amazing." Quinn took a step closer, smiled.

"You're a great mayor, Sutton. The best we've ever had and exactly what this town needs."

Touched more than she would have imagined, Sutton blinked back tears. It felt good to hear those words. "Thanks for saying that. It means..." she swallowed back a wave of emotion "...it really means a lot, especially coming from you."

"I'm sorry I waited so long to say what I've known to be true for some time."

They shared a smile.

Then Sutton sighed as a thought came to her. "It would be remiss of me not to point out that your brother isn't nearly as pleased as you are with my push to make Thunder Ridge a premier Christmas destination."

"Sadly, it's true. I can't deny it."

"What happened to him, Quinn? What turned Casey off the holiday?"

"I'm not sure, exactly. All I know is that a couple of years ago he was in a serious relationship and—" She abruptly stopped talking, shook her head. "Not my story to tell. And anyway, Casey seems to be coming around, slowly if not completely. That's another thing I can happily lay at your feet."

Sutton's heart kicked hard, wishing she could take the credit, knowing she couldn't. "Not me, Toby." Her voice sounded tight even to her own ears, probably because she was fixated on Quinn's revelation about Casey's *serious relationship.* "Your brother and my son have really bonded over the derby."

"I noticed. Anyway..." Quinn smoothly changed the subject. "How do you think we're doing in the contest, overall?"

Sutton lifted a shoulder. "Hard to know without more information."

"What have you heard?"

"Not much. I did check out the competition's website, but other than a list of events, corresponding dates and a few random pictures there wasn't much there. I have no idea how we're stacking up against Village Green, or they with us."

A shrewd look came into the other woman's eyes. "Maybe someone should make the fifty-mile drive around the mountain and check out the competition."

The thought had already occurred to Sutton. "I hear there's a lovely tearoom that serves brunch during the week."

Quinn grinned. "You could try it out. You know, see what all the fuss is about."

"I could do that."

"Want some company?"

It was Sutton's turn to grin. "Are you offering?"

"I am."

"Then, yes. Let's do it. Let's check out the competition." They made plans to meet outside City Hall at nine o'clock the next morning.

The school bell buzzed, jolting their attention to the front of the building. Within seconds, swarms of schoolchildren spilled out the front door. Toby exited with a large pack of boys and girls his age, including Samson and Quinn's twin daughters. One by one, kids peeled off from the group and sped toward a waiting car.

Toby looked around, then his gaze converged with Sutton's. A smile split his face. He said something to Samson and rushed ahead of his friend. "Hey, Mom." He peered inside the car. "You're alone?"

"I am."

"But it's Wednesday. I thought Mr. Casey picked me up on Wednesdays."

"He does, usually. But he got held up. Don't worry. He'll be at his house by the time we get there."

The little boy lurched up from his slouch. "Okay, cool."

She opened the door for him to scramble into the back seat and then made her way around to the driver's side of the car. She'd barely pulled away from the curb when Toby began regaling her with the news of his day. "Almost every boy in my class and half the girls have either entered the derby or are working on a team. I didn't know girls could enter."

Sutton bristled, but in the spirit of a teachable moment, made herself speak calmly. "Why wouldn't girls be able to enter?"

"I don't know. It's, well, cars and stuff." She opened her mouth to explain that girls were just as capable as boys, but her son was talking again. "It makes sense, though. Right? Cause, you know, if a girl can be mayor of a whole town then a girl can build a car."

Sutton sighed. She loved her son. She really, really did. "That's exactly right, Toby. Exactly right."

"Most of the kids have been working on their cars a lot longer than me. But Mr. Casey says we're not behind or anything, which is a good thing, I guess. You know? I think Mr. Casey is my favorite adult, ever, well, besides you and Grandpa." He took a breath. "Oh, and Samson's uncle, I like him too because he's a sheriff and I like Reno because he's going to teach me how to ski, if it's okay with you." He took another, quicker breath. "Or maybe Mr. Casey can teach me. He said he knew how. I asked. He said he had to run it by you first. Has he brought it up yet? Because I think I'd really like skiing. You like skiing, don't you, Mom?"

Trying desperately to keep up with her son's rambling, Sutton turned onto the highway leading to Casey's house and caught sight of Toby's face in the rearview mirror. "I definitely like skiing."

"Oh, good. Then it's okay if I learn?"

There was such joy in her son's voice, Sutton's stomach fluttered with emotion, a mixture of happiness and sorrow. Happiness for all she would share with her son as he grew up to be a man, sorrow for Jeremy, who would miss out on so much. She had to swallow several times to dislodge the lump in her throat. "I guess it's okay, yeah."

"When?"

"Soon. This winter, for sure. But you're going to need the proper gear first."

"You mean like skis and stuff?"

"Like skis and stuff." All of which would be a perfect Christmas gift for a seven-year-old boy. Much better than, oh, say, a puppy.

"Can we go to The Slippery Slope now?"

"Not now. You have a car to build."

"Oh, yeah." He laughed. "Can you maybe go a little faster? I really want to get there."

Sutton checked the speedometer, saw that she was driving a few miles under the speed limit. Realizing she wanted to get to Casey's as much as her son did, she pressed on the gas pedal as she said, "I can go a little faster."

\* \* \*

Not long after Sutton dropped Toby off, and then left again for a meeting that could go long— her words—Casey decided this was his chance to follow up on the promise he'd made to the boy. After he cleared out the garage. "And that's a wrap," he said to the two older men hovering near the unfinished car and discussing paint colors.

He didn't know who was more shocked by his pronouncement. Beau or Horace. "Wait. You're saying we're finished for the day?" Beau asked for the pair of them.

"That's what I'm saying."

"But it's early yet."

A truth Casey couldn't deny. "I'm taking Toby into town for some Christmas shopping." He paused to eye the boy playing with puppies on the other side of the garage. "He wants to pick out something special for his mom."

Expecting Sutton's father to push back—Toby was, after all, his grandson—Casey was surprised to see a spark of pleasure in the older man's eyes. "How'd the kid rope you into that thankless task?"

"I volunteered." Casey angled his head. "You're not upset, Beau?"

"Upset? Not at all. I think it's great you're taking the boy shopping." He grinned at Sutton's uncle. "Right, Horace?"

Horace nodded. "Really great."

Casey wasn't sure what to think of their over-the-top enthusiasm. Or why both men kept smiling and nodding, even as they packed up their tools and headed for the door. They must really hate shopping, he decided, maybe even more than Casey. Hard to imagine, but it certainly explained their odd behavior. "We'll pick up where we left off tomorrow," he called after them.

"We'll be here."

Toby kept up a running monologue on their way into town. The boy continued chatting as Casey guided him out of the truck and down Main Street. The sidewalk was swarming with holiday shoppers, many of whom carried Cargo Coffee bags. Ebenezer Grinch approved. "Any idea what you want to get your mom for Christmas?"

Toby shrugged. "I don't know. Maybe a candle or something? I heard girls like candles."

"Sure they do. But I think we can do better than that." Or rather, Casey knew someone who could help them do better. As the older brother of two discerning sisters, he'd learned long ago to throw himself at the mercy of an expert when it came to gift giving.

Plan in place, he escorted Toby into the first, and hopefully last, shop of the afternoon. According to his sisters, The Sweet Pea Bumble Bee was *the place* to buy a special gift for a woman. Bonus, the owner, Francine Finch, was both a good friend of Quinn's and had dated McCoy on and off for years.

Inside the store, Toby looked around, eyes wide and flooded with little-boy trepidation. "There's a lot of girl stuff in here."

*That* was an understatement. "Since your mom's a girl, I'm thinking we're in the right place."

"If you say so."

It took Casey less than two seconds to discover Francine was working with another customer. He was just about to call in the troops, aka one or both of his sisters, when she saw him, smiled and broke away to head in his direction. "Hey, Casey."

"Hey, Francine."

Her eyes lingered on his face a moment longer, then slowly dropped to Toby. "And who might this be?"

"This is Toby Wentworth. The mayor's son. We're looking for a very special Christmas gift for his mom."

"Actually, we're looking for two gifts," Toby corrected. "One from me, and one from Mr. Casey because they're good friends and he likes my mom almost as much as I do."

Francine's gaze lit with interest. "Oh, he does, does he?"

"Yep, he likes her a lot. Everybody knows it."

"I see." Francine winked at Casey, asked Toby a few questions, and his general price range, then began steering the boy through the store.

Happy to hand over the reins, Casey wandered around on his own. A display of multicolored scarfs caught his eye. "Hey, Toby, look at these." He randomly plucked one off the table. "What do you think?"

The boy considered the option with a thoughtful expression. "My mom has a lot of them already. Hey, what are those?"

Casey studied the trio of glass bottles the boy pointed out. "Not a clue."

"They're olive oil pourers," Francine said, coming up behind Toby. "Handblown by a local artist whose inspiration came from his recent trip to Greece."

Toby moved in closer. "They're really pretty."

"They definitely look like something your mom would like." They were also way out of the kid's price range. Francine opened her mouth, probably to say that very thing, but Casey shook his head.

Toby reached out, stopped himself, swung his gaze up to Casey. "What do you think? Should I get them for her?"

"You should. We'll take all three," Casey said to Francine. "You giftwrap?"

She smiled. "You know I do."

While she went to work, Toby offered to help Casey find something he could give Sutton. This task proved much harder and the boy soon grew bored. He wandered over to a table of jewelry, fiddled with a pair of earrings, sighed, went to another table and sighed again, the sound both sad and desperate.

Casey felt his response in the quickening of his heart rate. "What's wrong, Toby?"

"I... I'm worried Mom is gonna cry at Christmas again, like she did last year." Dropping his hand, he rolled those big, brown, innocent eyes up to Casey. "She tried to hide it from me, but I knew. I cried, too, cause I was missing my dad."

Casey's gut twisted so hard he had to swallow to catch his breath. "I'm sorry you and your mom were sad."

Toby heaved another sigh. "I used to really worry about her, but she said I didn't have to because a mom is supposed to worry about her son, not the other way around."

That sounded like Sutton. "Your mom loves you very much."

"I know. I love her, too." Toby went silent for a moment, lost in his own private thoughts. "She doesn't cry anymore. I don't hardly cry, either, only sometimes, when I miss my dad."

The kid might as well have reached inside his

chest and ripped out his heart. Throat thick, the back of his eyes burning, Casey smoothed a hand over the bent head. "I miss your dad, too. He was a good man."

He would never disparage Jeremy in the eyes of his son.

"Mom says the same thing, like all the time." Toby wandered over to another table.

Casey followed him. "Have you thought about what you want for Christmas?"

"Oh, I think about it all the time." Toby's eyes settled on Casey with a clarity that gave him a bad feeling in the pit of his stomach. "I want a new dad."

Stepped right into that one. "You want a new dad," he repeated.

"Not to replace mine, or anything, because I'll always love him, like for forever, but that doesn't mean I can't get a new dad like Samson did when he moved into his uncle's house."

"You want a new dad," Casey croaked out again.

"Well, yeah. That's what I said. And then that would mean…" Toby chewed furiously on his bottom lip, his seven-year-old brain working through the logic. "My mom would get a new husband, right?"

The kid was killing him. "That's usually how it works."

"If I got a new dad and she got a new husband that would make Mom really happy."

The wistful look in Toby's eyes shot past every defense Casey had erected since his breakup with Victoria. Something stirred inside him, something strong and lasting. A desperate need to fulfill Toby's wish?

Impossible, on nearly every level. Too many lies and secrets stood between Casey and Sutton. In situations such as these, the best response was good old-fashioned deflection. "What else is on your Christmas list?"

"Oh, that's easy." Toby answered without hesitation. "There's only one other gift I want."

"Which is…?"

"A bulldog puppy named Louie."

# Chapter Eleven

Casey's day started at four the following morning in his home gym. He pushed himself through the workout. His body responded with practiced ease. His mind was a different matter. His thoughts chased around in circles, nearly spinning out before landing in a hard skid on Toby's Christmas wish.

*I want a new dad.*

Casey almost smiled. Almost, but not quite. Though Toby hadn't said the words out loud, it was obvious who the boy wanted to fill the position. Casey wanted it, too. He wanted to marry Sutton and be Toby's father in every way.

Was it possible? Could he and Sutton find a way back to each other and build a future together? Last night, he'd thought no. This morning, his mind kept falling firmly in the maybe camp. And only if he went against his word and ratted out a friend. Just like that, a gloom settled over him and he paused to wipe the sweat out of his eyes before moving through a series of bicep curls.

Longing wanted to overwhelm him. Barely two weeks in her company, Sutton was back in his heart and Victoria was a thing in the past. Outwardly, Casey was no different. On the inside, he was permanently altered. For better or for worse?

Too soon to tell.

He was still puzzling over the question as he showered and dressed for an early-morning puppy delivery to a family living in Village Green. While he was there, he would stop in at his second location of Cargo Coffee. That meant leaving the other dogs at home, including his best pal, Winston. The animal accepted his fate with a long-suffering sigh that cut Casey to the bone.

"Sorry, old friend." He rubbed the dog's head. "I've ignored my other coffee shop too many days in a row. I need to see what's what." His manager claimed all was good. The spreadsheets and financials presented a similar picture, but it never hurt to put eyes on the situation.

Casey poured fresh-brewed coffee in a travel mug, secured the recently weaned puppy in a carrier, and hustled out to the garage. He contemplated his choices, then decided the '63 Mustang needed airing out more than the Goat.

With the puppy carrier fastened in the back

seat, Casey flipped on the heater, put the car in gear and then pulled out of the garage. Halfway up the drive, he pressed on the brake and studied his home in the dawn's early-morning light. Sutton was right. He'd done a pitiful job of decorating, all because of an old resentment he should have let go a long time ago.

The house deserved better. He'd purchased it with Victoria in mind, or so he'd told himself. Now Casey wondered if his own dream of raising a large family on the property had colored his decision. Victoria had never liked the house. According to her, it was too big, with too much wood and glass, and entirely too far from town.

What she'd really meant was that the house had too much Casey in it.

He closed his eyes and waited for the familiar slice of pain to come with the memory of her harsh words. When his heart remained unmoved, he opened his eyes and looked back at the house. This time, the image of another woman filled his mind. Shoulder-length blond hair, blue eyes, long legs, the loving mother of a remarkable kid. The yearning came again. Like before, he let it come, rode with it all the way to Village Green.

The puppy drop-off went well. He met the couple at the husband's place of business because, unlike the Denver family, this one wanted to surprise their son on Christmas Day. While the wife was cooing over the baby bulldog, the husband reached out his hand. "Thank you, Mr. Evans. You've made our little boy very happy."

"Glad to hear it." He meant every word. Ebenezer Grinch was going soft.

So soft, in fact, that when he arrived at the second Cargo Coffee location, he mentally compared the building's decorations to its counterpart in Thunder Ridge. Shelby, his manager, had done a decent job. She'd even added garland along with the colorful lights, but the end result was nothing compared to what Sutton had pulled off.

A sense of fairness clamored through his blood. Could he, in good conscience, allow one of his locations to outdo the other? Didn't seem right.

Casey dug his cell phone out of his pocket and texted Emory with what she probably considered an odd request. He had to give her points for not asking why he wanted a picture of the exterior of the coffee shop, or why he wanted it ASAP. Five minutes later, his phone dinged with an incoming text. Emory had come through for him.

The moment he enlarged the image, Casey's suspicions were confirmed. Oh, yeah. Cargo Coffee's Thunder Ridge location looked entirely more festive and Christmassy than the Village Green version. That, he decided, could not stand. If Thunder Ridge won the contest, it had to be on a level playing field or it wouldn't really count.

Unable to let it go until he at least *tried* to fix the discrepancy, he texted his manager to meet him outside on the sidewalk. Shelby arrived looking harried, distracted and nearly out of breath. "What's up?"

He took in the disheveled apron, messy ponytail and realized he'd pulled her away at a bad time. "Never mind, you're busy. I'll take care of it myself."

"Really? You're going to leave me hanging like that?" She jammed a fist on her right hip. "You called me outside for a reason and I want to know why."

"The building needs more Christmas decorations." Whoa, did that just come out of his mouth? Casey inwardly groaned. Ebenezer Grinch wasn't going soft. He'd melted into a pool of greasy carburetor oil.

"You want *more* decorations?" Shelby angled her head and ran her gaze over the building. "Like how much more?"

"Like this much." He thumbed open the screen on his phone and showed her the picture Emory had just sent.

"Wow, that looks great. Seriously awesome. But…" She lifted her head. "I don't know if I can recreate that. I mean." Frowning, she looked back down. "It's pretty extensive and it would require a trip to the store for more decorations and supplies."

"Like I said before, I'm not asking you. I'm going to do it. *After* I help you with the morning crush."

Relief showed in her eyes. "I could use another pair of hands. The crowd is pretty big."

Music to his ears. "Then we better get to it."

Quinn cut the engine of her ridiculously large SUV and swiveled in her seat to face Sutton directly. "You ready for this?"

"Nearly." Sutton shoved the oversized sunglasses on her face, straightened the beanie with the two puffs on top, then nodded. "Now I'm ready."

"Me, too."

Wearing a similar disguise, the other woman reached for the door handle. Sutton stopped her with a hand on her arm. "Quinn, wait."

Two eyebrows shot up over the rim of the oversize sunglasses. "Having second thoughts?"

"No, I just…hang on." She took off her own sunglasses. "I want to thank you for agreeing to come with me this morning. It matters."

"Of course, it matters. I am totally up for whatever it takes to win the magazine contest. Well, within the bounds of the rules, of course." She grinned. "And there is nothing that says two savvy women can't enjoy brunch and a little shopping in a neighboring town."

"True." Sutton tried to return the other woman's smile, but feared she fell short. She had jitters tangled around jitters. "But that's not what I meant."

Quinn nodded. "I know. I was trying to lighten the mood before we dredged up the past."

"Valiant effort."

"I thought so." She gave a little laugh, then grew serious. "We're doing this now?"

"I guess we are."

"Okay. I'll start." Quinn took off her sunglasses and set them on the dashboard behind the steering wheel. "What happened between you and Casey back in high school, the way it all went down, it left a lot of hurt people in its wake. I'm including myself in that number."

"I know and I'm sorry for that. I didn't just lose Casey. I lost you, too. You were my best friend. I've missed you every day since."

"And I've missed you."

"But…?"

Quinn took a deep, shuddering breath. "What I never understood… Honestly, what I still don't understand, is why you so easily accepted that Casey would bring beer to your party."

"What was I supposed to think? He confessed."

"Sure, he confessed. A little too quickly, don't

you think? I mean, he was seventeen. And yeah, even back then he had a strong moral compass. But come on—" Quinn shook her head "—where was his sense of self-preservation? He didn't even try to squirm out of it. He gave no excuses, no evasive answers, just, '*I did it, Sheriff Michaels. I brought the beer.*'"

Letting Quinn's words sink in, processing every one of them, all true, Sutton closed her eyes and leaned her head back against the car seat.

"I think Casey was covering for someone," Quinn said into the silence.

"I thought that, too, at first." Sutton opened her eyes. "I desperately wanted to believe he'd acted on behalf of someone else. But I asked him if he was taking the blame for a friend. He refused to answer. He just shut me out."

Quinn sighed. "I never understood that, either."

Seeking some new revelation, Sutton continued telling her side of the story. "When Casey refused to talk to me, I went to Jeremy."

"What did he say?"

"That Casey brought the beer."

"Hmm." Quinn reached for her sunglasses but didn't put them on her face. "I'm still not convinced he did. Casey knew your history, Sutton. He knew how you felt about alcohol and why. I can't believe he'd dishonor you like that. He loved you too much."

But had he, really? Sutton felt the sting of bitter tears in her eyes, remembering the way he'd pulled away from her so completely. "I keep coming back to one undeniable truth. Casey confessed. He signed a statement. Took the community service. What was I supposed to think if not that he'd been the one to bring the beer?"

"I guess, for me, that was never the issue." Quinn held Sutton's stare, her own eyes filling with tears. "I always thought you would stand by him, no matter what."

"I—" Sutton searched for the words to defend herself, but there was really only one response. "You're right, Quinn. I should have stood by him, no matter what. But I didn't and we broke up. I lost the love of my life and my best friend, and now, here we are, sitting in a parking lot a block away from Village Green's town center, both of us on the verge of tears."

"Here we are, indeed."

She took her friend's hand and held on tight. "I'm sorry I hurt you, Quinn. Sorrier than I can ever put into words. Can you forgive me?"

"Of course I forgive you and I'm going to ask the same of you."

Sutton smiled. "I forgave you years ago."

The hug they shared across the center console was physically awkward but just as healing had they been standing on the sidewalk.

"Well, then," Quinn said, sitting back, "now that we're both entirely too sad and emotional to be of any use to anyone, what do you say we set aside the past and do a little recon for our hometown?"

Sutton liked that idea. "I'm down with that."

As if they were a pair of synchronized swimmers, they shoved their sunglasses in place, adjusted their scarves and hats, then exited the vehicle as a single unit. Sutton's stomach dipped to her toes. Thunder Ridge had some serious competition in Village Green. Main Street looked like a picture postcard, with sparkles and color everywhere. Fat, lazy snowflakes fell over the heavily decorated buildings. Wreaths adorned the streetlamps, while miles of Christmas lights and garland hung from every available ledge, roofline and storefront window.

Including… Was that…?

She narrowed her eyes at the building across the street. "Casey opened a second location of Cargo Coffee?"

"Six months ago. You didn't know?"

How would she know? It wasn't as if she was Casey's confidante anymore. She felt another punch when the man himself exited the building, carrying several shopping bags from a big-box store. He set them down on the sidewalk, consulted something on his phone, nodded, then began pulling out Christmas lights. He pulled out a staple gun next and…

"Is he decorating?"

"Now, Sutton," Quinn said in a slow, calming voice. "Let's not overreact. I'm sure there's a logical explanation."

She was too stunned to think clearly, or logically. She took off across the street, barely checking for traffic, uncaring if Quinn followed her or not. By the time she completed the journey, her frustration bubbled over into outrage. "How could you?"

"Sutton?" Casey glanced up from the bag, his face free of guilt, of remorse, of anything but mild curiosity. "What are you doing here?"

"The question is what are *you* doing here?" She whipped off her sunglasses and glared at the box of multicolored lights in his hand. "Are you deliberately trying to sabotage me?"

"What are you talking about? Sabotage you how?" The man seemed genuinely baffled.

He was also close, close enough to force her to tilt her head to look into his eyes. What she saw was the confusion swirling in their depths, in the twist of his lips. He hadn't shaved. The dark stubble on his jaw was disconcerting. And attractive. Oh no. She would not let that handsome face distract her.

"I can't believe you're decorating your coffee

shop in Village Green when you refused, *refused*, to do the same in Thunder Ridge. I can only assume this—" she waved her hand at the building "—is your way of ensuring I fail."

"You think this—" he too waved his hand at the building "—is about you?"

"The evidence speaks for itself."

"Trust me, Sutton, my issues with Christmas have absolutely nothing to do with you."

She wanted to believe him. Quinn had mentioned something about a previous relationship, the details of which he'd kept to himself. More shutting her out, Sutton realized. More distance. Why did the man have to be so close-lipped about everything? Why couldn't he just speak plainly, openly? Because whoever the woman was, she'd hurt him badly.

"Sutton." Quinn moved in beside her, touched her arm. "We should go inside or do this later. You're drawing a crowd."

She knew it. At the moment, she didn't much care. Later, she would. Right now, the man owed her an explanation. "Help me understand why, Casey. Why are you blatantly trying to torpedo Thunder Ridge's chances at winning the contest?"

"Decorating both of my stores in an identical manner isn't torpedoing anybody's chances. It isn't sabotage. It's simply the right thing to do. The fair thing to do."

"And that's all you're going to say on the matter?"

"It's the simple truth."

She blew out a frustrated breath. "This is high school all over again."

"I guess it is," he said grimly. "Because once again you're assigning motives to my behavior that just aren't there. I'm telling you my intentions are good, but you're incapable of giving me the benefit of the doubt."

"And you're incapable of trusting me enough to tell me the truth, all of it, not some watered-down version that leaves more questions than answers."

"I told you everything you need to know. This—" another careless hand wave toward the building "—is about fairness."

"Fairness," she repeated.

"That's right. If—*when*—Thunder Ridge wins the contest, it won't be because I played favorites. How can you not see that?"

Sutton opened her mouth to argue, but he had a point. A very valid point. She tried to tell him that, but he'd turned his back, dismissing her and their conversation. She sighed. They'd been here before. She'd get nothing more out of him this morning.

Evidently coming to the same conclusion, Quinn

linked their arms together and, with much patience, guided her down the sidewalk. "Let's go home, Sutton."

She let her friend lead her away. Back in the SUV, silence reigned. Now that Sutton had time to think logically, she understood what Casey was doing. Her suspicions were confirmed when he kept looking down at his phone and then back up at the building, as if comparing his efforts to something on the screen. It took less than a nanosecond to realize he was attempting to duplicate what she herself had done to his building in Thunder Ridge. His sense of fairness had trumped his own personal issues with Christmas.

This was partly her fault.

If she'd misread his motives today, had she misread them seventeen years ago? "Casey was right," she said on a sigh. "I don't know him at all."

"You know him."

Did she? Sutton thought about Casey's love for his dogs, his sense of humor and penchant for playing pranks via a plastic Santa. She thought about his endless stores of patience, not only with Toby but with his employees, his nieces and nephews, his brothers and sisters. And then there was the way he'd kept in touch with her father through the years and had maintained a strong relationship with her uncle, the man who'd arrested him. "I owe him an apology."

"You do," Quinn agreed. "But not now. He's pretty steamed and you need to cool off, too."

Truer words were never spoken. But Sutton wouldn't be denied. A text message wasn't the best solution. And yet, she pulled out her phone and began to type anyway. I'm sorry. I overreacted. You were right. I was wrong. Truce?

He left her waiting only seconds. Her heart jolted pleasantly as she read his response. Truce. Then... Dinner's on you tonight.

She could live with that.

Only fair, she typed, then added: Prepare to be amazed.

# Chapter Twelve

Despite agreeing to Sutton's request for a truce, Casey spent the rest of the morning rehashing their argument. His mind kept sticking on one specific accusation she'd thrown at him. *You're incapable of trusting me enough to tell me the truth.*

She was wrong. Casey's silence had nothing to do with trust and everything to do with his promise to Jeremy. At eighteen, an arrest would have gone on his friend's permanent record and nullified his scholarship to the Air Force Academy. Still a minor, Casey had been brought before the juvenile courts. His record had been sealed and the incident permanently expunged after he'd completed his community service.

Casey's loyalty to Jeremy extended to his son. Toby had captured his heart and made him want to do right by the boy. Pulling his attention to the here and now, he arrived home to find Horace Michaels waiting for him on his front porch. After a quick glance around, Casey climbed out of the Mustang and asked, "Toby and Beau aren't with you?"

"The kid was hungry, so they stopped at the Latte Da for burgers and fries. That stays between us." Horace pointed a finger at him. "Don't tell Sutton."

"Tell Sutton what?"

"Good man. Anyway." Looking very much like the law enforcement officer he'd once been, Horace gave Casey a thorough once-over. "I came on ahead because I wanted to speak with you alone."

"All right. But I need to let the dogs out first."

By the time Winston, Clementine and one rowdy puppy named Louie were outside kicking up snow, the former sheriff's impatience was a living, breathing thing. "What's going on, Horace? You seem agitated about something."

The older man looked over his shoulder, as if checking to see if they were truly alone. "I've noticed you and my niece are spending a lot of time together again."

Casey blew out a breath. "Wow, Horace, you haven't lost your powers of observation."

The other man jagged a thumb at himself. "Not just a pretty face."

Since the former sheriff resembled Winston on

a good day, Casey decided to keep quiet. Quiet was good. Quiet meant he couldn't trip up and say something he shouldn't.

Apparently, Horace wasn't a fellow card-carrying member of the silence-is-golden club. "I've also noticed that you and Sutton seem to be getting along pretty good."

Casey said nothing. Because, yeah, sure, they were getting along, if a person didn't count their argument this morning, or their ongoing prank war over a plastic Santa, or just about every other interaction they'd had in the past two weeks.

"But I would venture," Horace continued, "that it hasn't always been smooth sailing, and I blame myself."

That unhooked Casey's jaw real fast. "Come again?"

"I said…" Crossing his arms over his chest, Horace leaned against the porch railing. "I blame myself for the tension that occasionally shows up between you and Sutton."

Casey moved to the steps leading to his front yard, sat, stretched out his legs. "Whatever tension that exists between Sutton and me is firmly on the two of us, not you."

"Disagree." Horace joined him on the step, maintaining eye contact as he settled in. "I should have pressed you harder during my interrogation the night I arrested you."

It hadn't been much of an interrogation. "Press for what? I was pretty clear in my confession. I gave details. Lots of them." Most of them true. "I even produced receipts."

"*Cash* receipts. Not exactly compelling evidence. Nor was your confession, for that matter. Your story had a big gaping hole the size of the Grand Canyon."

Casey saw no reason to respond.

"You do realize I could have cracked you like a squirrel with a brittle nut."

A trickle of sweat slid down his back. Nope, still not talking.

"Almost from the start, I understood what you were up to, which is why I made sure your record was sealed and then expunged. What you did was noble, boy. Misguided, but noble."

Casey picked up the ball at his feet and threw it for the puppy. "I stand by my confession."

"Don't patronize me, Casey. I may be retired, but I'm still a seasoned lawman with hundreds of arrests to my name. And you, my young friend, still can't look me in the eye. It's a blatant tell."

"I'm not avoiding eye contact." Head down, Casey wrestled the ball from the animal's mouth and threw it again. "I'm exercising the puppy."

"Uh-huh. You should tell Sutton what really happened that night."

To what end? It wouldn't bring Jeremy back.

It wouldn't change the past. All it would do was ruin Sutton's memory of the man she'd married, and possibly teach Toby that his father had lied to his mother their entire marriage.

"You hear me, boy?"

"I heard you."

"Well? You gonna tell my niece the truth?"

Casey was saved from responding when Beau's car drove into view. The vehicle barely rolled to a stop before Toby-the-Tornado exited the back seat and zipped in their direction. All three dogs perked up. Louie, despite his short little legs and youthful clumsiness, set out ahead of his parents.

Laughing, Toby fell onto the snow-covered ground and let the little guy climb all over him. Not to be denied their piece of the action, Winston and Clementine piled on.

*This*, Casey thought, *this is what I want. A family, a wife, and at least one little boy who loves rolling around in the snow with my dogs.*

That life could be his. If, as Horace suggested, he told her the truth about that night, maybe he and Sutton could—

He cut off the rest of his thoughts.

Nothing had changed. For whatever reason, Jeremy chose to take his secret to the grave. Casey would honor his friend's decision the only way he knew how. With his continued silence.

\* \* \*

Sutton read Casey's text. Toby and I are finished up here. Expect us for dinner around 6:00.

So he was holding her to her promise, after all. Good. They needed to put the past behind them. Tonight would be the night. After she'd plied Casey with his favorite meal.

Sutton was putting the finishing touches on the lasagna when the front door swung open with a bang and her son shouted from the entryway. "Hey, Mom. Mom! Where are you? I have super exciting news."

"I'm back here," she called out. "In the kitchen."

Expecting to see Toby speed through the doorway, she nearly dropped the spatula when her eyes connected with Casey's. A small part of her brain functioned normally. The rest gathered details, the whiff of motor oil, the intense blueness of his eyes, the smile that didn't quite reach them. "I know that smell," he said by way of a greeting. "Please tell me you made lasagna."

"Not only that. I'm using your mother's recipe."

"Be still my heart. Wait." He lifted an eyebrow. "Are you trying to bribe me?"

"Consider it an olive branch." Remembering how he hated olives, she quickly added, "Sans the olives."

This time, his smile reached his eyes. "Nice recovery."

"I know!" They had a private moment of understanding, broken by Toby's shriek of delight as he sped into the kitchen. "We're having lasagna? That's my favorite."

Casey squeezed the boy's shoulder. "Same, little man. Same."

Toby grinned up at the man who had clearly become his hero. "This is almost my very favorite day, ever. All that's missing is a puppy of my very own."

"Nice try, kiddo." Sutton picked up a spatula. "The answer is still no."

"Aw, Mom." Looking down, Toby scuffed his foot on the tile floor. "Louie is a great dog. He's really well-behaved. He'd be no trouble at all."

Patently untrue. But instead of arguing with her son, she attempted to redirect the boy's focus. "Wasn't there some super exciting news you wanted to tell me?"

"Oh, yeah." Toby's head popped up. "We finished my car today!"

"No kidding?" She posed the question to Casey. "That was quick work. I'm impressed."

"Don't be. We had a team of highly motivated workers."

Sutton knew it was more than that. "You're a good leader, Casey. The air force lost a valuable asset when you retired. Ah, well, their loss is Thunder Ridge's gain."

He tilted his head. "Did you just pay me a compliment?"

"As real as they come. Now go wash your hands. Both of you." She pointed her spatula at her son, then Casey. "No dawdling."

"Yes, ma'am." The two saluted her. The move was so perfectly synchronized she wondered if they'd practiced it.

Dinner was a happy affair with lots of laughter.

It wasn't until after they ate, and Toby was in his room working on his homework, that Sutton brought up her argument with Casey. "I want to talk about what happened this morning."

Casey kept his face expressionless. "No need. You already apologized."

"In a text."

A frown line appeared between his dark eyebrows. "You asked for a truce. I accepted. It's over, Sutton. Leave it alone."

She moved closer, put a hand on his shoulder. "Please, Casey. Let me have my say."

After a moment, he nodded.

"I need to check on Toby first, then I'll make coffee and we'll talk in the living room."

"I'll make the coffee." Some of his previous humor returned. "I am, after all, an expert."

"You'll get no argument from you."

"Har har."

She patted his cheek. "I'll be right back."

When she returned, she found Casey in the living room, head bent, no coffee in sight. He held the framed photograph taken on her wedding day in his hand. They never talked about Jeremy. But he was always between them, hovering, the memory of him as real as if he were standing in the room. Sutton had no idea what Casey thought of her marrying his best friend. This was the perfect moment to find out.

She moved deeper into the room. Casey's shoulders stiffened, but he never took his eyes off the photograph in his hand. "You look beautiful in this picture. Happy."

"I was happy." She touched the gilded frame, smiling softly at the image of her and Jeremy. "I married my best friend that day."

Casey set the picture back on the mantel. "Was he a good husband and father?"

"Yes," she said with only a slight hesitation. "To both questions."

His eyes, a deep, searching blue, skimmed over her.

"Casey, I've always wondered…" She could barely form the words in her mind, but managed to speak them as they came to her. "What did you think when you found out Jeremy asked me to marry him, and that I said yes?"

He turned his attention back to the picture.

"We'd broken up years before you and Jeremy married."

"That's not an answer."

Emotion drained out of his face and a blank mask moved in. "What do you want me to say? That I was overjoyed with the news that my former girlfriend was marrying my best friend? That I wished you nothing but happiness?"

He didn't sound angry, exactly. He sounded hurt. "Is that how you felt? You wished Jeremy and me *nothing but happiness*?"

He shrugged. "Close enough."

"Casey, please. We need to talk about this."

"Why?"

Here it was. The moment of truth for them both. "Because we're growing close again. Something is building between us, something stronger than when we were kids."

He didn't deny it.

"But Jeremy is a part of my past and the father of my son. He will always be between us if we don't speak about him honestly."

"You want honesty from me? Then you give it first. Was Jeremy a good husband and father? Tell me the truth, Sutton."

She stared at him for five full seconds, not quite sure what she heard in his voice. It was as if Casey knew something about Jeremy that Sutton didn't, something that concerned him enough to ask a question she'd already answered.

"He was good to Toby and me. When he was home, which was rarely, because he took extra assignments whenever he could." The words flew out of her mouth and she couldn't take them back. "He loved his job. His dedication bordered on obsession."

*As if he had something to prove.* Where had that thought come from?

"Are you saying his career was more important than his family?"

"When you say it like that, it makes him sound neglectful. He wasn't. He was kind. But he was also driven. He had plans and goals and could be single-minded when it came to achieving them, often at the expense of his relationships."

"I'm sorry."

She drew in a quick breath. "All that time and sacrifice. All the lost days with Toby he won't have to enjoy. It's such a…" She left the rest unspoken, too choked up to continue. The tragedy of Jeremy's death wasn't just about her, but also her son. The loss that Toby suffered, it left her grasping for calm, and trying not to cry.

"I'm sorry, Sutton. So very sorry."

Sutton appreciated the absence of platitudes. "He died too young. But at least he died doing what he loved." She briefly closed her eyes, opened them again. "I find comfort in that."

"Then I will, too." He sounded as wounded as she felt. In that moment, she realized Casey had lost Jeremy, too, and the pain was just as raw for him as it was for her and Toby.

The tears came then, hot and fast, and she tried to turn away from Casey's intense gaze, but she couldn't. She didn't want to, didn't even try. She wanted to share her grief with someone who knew Jeremy as well as she.

She reached to Casey. He reached to her. And then they were in each other's arms. Her head on his shoulder. Their breathing erratic yet somehow also healing.

Casey's hand came up and he stroked her hair, the move of a friend and yet so much more intimate than had he kissed her. She had no idea how long they stood like that, wrapped tightly against one another, taking comfort in their mutual grief while letting go of the man they'd both loved, despite his flaws. Perhaps even because of them.

"Okay. In the spirit of honesty…" Casey said, setting her away from him. "I won't lie and say I wasn't hurt when I found out you married Jeremy. It hurt a lot. More than I cared to admit at the time, which probably explains why I…" He trailed off, shook his head.

When he remained silent, she touched the back of his hand. "Explains what?"

"Not important."

She sensed it *was* important, but Casey was talking again, and she'd lost her chance to press him. "I cared about you both, Sutton. And no matter how ugly things got between us, all I ever wanted was for you to be happy."

"It's that simple for you?"

"Simple? No. Easy? Not even close." He shrugged, the gesture as familiar today as it had been seventeen years ago. "It helped that I was in a serious relationship at the time. Knowing I had Victoria, and confident that we were good together, better than most couples I knew, well, that certainly took away some of the sting."

Victoria. Casey had been involved with a woman named Victoria. "Were you and… Victoria…" Her voice tripped over the woman's name. "How serious were you?"

"I planned to ask her to marry me."

"Oh." Sutton wasn't sure what else to say. The kick in her heart wasn't a pleasant feeling. "You loved her?"

"At the time, yes. I did. Like I said, we were good together. She was a pilot in the air force. That's how we met."

"You had a lot in common."

"We did, and we were of the same mind on

the important things." He rubbed a hand over his forehead. "Or so I thought."

Sutton saw it again, the look of regret in his eyes, and the hollowness underneath. "You were wrong?"

"We made plans to take our relationship to the next level once we were both out of the military. I left the air force ahead of her, at the end of June. She was supposed to join me here in Thunder Ridge six months later."

Sutton did the math in her head. "Just in time for Christmas."

He nodded. "I planned to ask her to marry me under the tree. I went all out with the decorations. But Victoria didn't make it for Christmas. She claimed there was a clerical error with her discharge paperwork."

*She claimed.* Two words that explained so much.

"One thing I learned in the military is to expect the unexpected, so it wasn't a big deal. I could wait. And that's what I did. I kept the decorations up and waited."

*Oh, Casey.*

"When she finally showed up in early February, she told me there'd been no clerical error. She'd had a change of heart but didn't know how to break the news to me." A shadow crossed over his face. "She returned to the air force, her one true love. I threw out the Christmas tree and vowed never to celebrate the holiday again."

Sutton's heart constricted as she looked into the kind, handsome face. She noted the "no big deal" expression that was a brave front but certainly not the truth. The breakup had left him wounded. No wonder Quinn was so protective of him. No wonder Remy had dubbed him Ebenezer Grinch.

"Oh, Casey, if I'd known I wouldn't have pushed you so hard to decorate your shop."

The smile he gave her was full of the boy she'd once known. "We both know that's not true. Putting Thunder Ridge on the list of top ten Christmas destinations is important to you."

She sighed deeply, because he was absolutely correct. "True, but I would have approached the situation with more delicacy."

"I don't want your pity."

"Understanding is not pity."

He almost smiled.

"For what it's worth," Sutton ventured, "Victoria made a huge mistake letting you go. Huge. Colossal. Massive. Ginormous."

He did smile then. "You buy yourself a word-of-the-day calendar, or did you confiscate mine?"

"Thesaurus, actually."

He laughed, the sound a reminder of another time. She could still remember the boy he'd been.

The laughter and the smiles meant only for her. The way she felt when their eyes met across a classroom, a gym floor, a football field. Life, even with her struggles at home, had been easy back then. Simple. But also fragile, and over too soon.

And their life together might possibly be over for good if they didn't settle the past here and now. They'd talked about Jeremy and a woman named Victoria, but they'd skirted around the bigger issue that stood between them. "Since we're bearing our hearts, let me say this before I lose my nerve. I was wrong, Casey. I should have stood by you after your arrest. I should have looked beyond the circumstantial evidence and trusted there was a reason why you confessed."

Something powerful came and went in his eyes, something like hope, but then his gaze went blank. "I…thank you for saying that, Sutton."

"It's the truth. I let you down. For that, I'm truly sorry."

"I'm sorry, too. I'm sorry I shut you out. But I can't tell you anything more about that night than I already have."

*Can't.* Not *won't*, but *can't.* The distinction was important. She knew that now, understood it on a molecular level. "I'm not asking you to betray your friend."

"You're not asking me to…what? *What* did you just say?"

"I know you were covering for someone. No. Don't deny it. I've done a lot of thinking about this. It's the only explanation that makes sense."

"You seem pretty certain."

"That's because I know you, Casey." She gave him a soft smile. "I know that any time you do something bad it's for something good. Like the time you painted Mrs. Corbin's window black to keep that bird from slamming into it again."

A ghost of a smile crossed his lips. "She was really mad."

"But the bird lived. Because of you."

There it was again, that glimmer of hope in his eyes.

"Casey, I know your heart and I know your character, so I'm not going to ask you to give me a name because I know you can't."

"I made a promise." The look he gave her was full of despair.

Images of Jeremy tried to intrude. Sutton parried and sidestepped. Not yet. Not ever. Casey couldn't have been covering for Jeremy. He would have told her. He'd had years to confess, first as her friend, then as her husband. Who, then, had Casey been protecting? Another friend? One of his siblings?

Casey's watch dinged with an alert. He lifted his arm and read the tiny text. "I need to make a call."

"Do you want privacy?"

He shook his head, already dragging his phone out of his pocket and swiping open the screen. The conversation lasted less than a minute. Sutton caught enough to know there was an accident and a rural hospital needed several pints of rare blood flown in from Denver. "I have to head out."

"Let me walk you to your car."

They stood beside the Mustang, the past and the present converging into this moment. "Well," she said, her voice low and weary. "It's certainly been a day of revelations."

"And forgiveness."

"That, too."

He reached for her, hooked his arm around her shoulders, pulled her against him. "A long time coming, wouldn't you say?"

"I do." She leaned into him. "It's nice, this. Being in your arms again." She burrowed deeper into his embrace. "It feels good. It feels—"

"Right," he said, finishing her sentence as he lifted a hand and cupped her face. "You were right, Sutton, About us. There is something here. Something stronger than before. Something worth exploring."

"Yes."

He dipped his head. "You should put a stop to this," he said softly.

She lifted up on her toes and whispered, "Kiss me, Casey."

He brushed his mouth over hers. He kept the kiss brief, then stood back. Smiling, he reached down, tugged at the hem of his jeans and inspected something near his shoe. "Huh."

Sutton made a sound deep in her throat. "What?"

"Just checking something."

"Checking what?"

"Pretty sure that kiss just blew my socks off. Wait. No. My mistake." He straightened, grinned with all his boyish charm. "They're still firmly on my feet."

How she loved this man's sense of humor. "You big weirdo."

Reaching up, she grabbed the lapels of his leather jacket and tugged him to her. She didn't say another word for a very long time. She let her kiss do the talking.

# Chapter Thirteen

The city council scheduled the Torchlight Parade exactly two weeks before the travel magazine's announcement of their contest winner. The popular event was what Casey considered Thunder Ridge's big chance to pull ahead of Village Green. Once the sun went down in a few hours, hundreds of skiers would crisscross down the slopes while carrying road flares. The mountain would come alive with light. Fireworks would follow. And, if everything went according to plan, a plastic Santa would make a surprise appearance sometime during the festivities.

Casey had a solid plan.

Unfortunately, with the event hours away yet, and Toby still in school, and Cargo Coffee fully staffed, Casey also had too much free time on his hands. He could tackle the mountain of paperwork piling up on his desk or he could walk over to City Hall and bug Sutton. He liked the last idea way better than the first. He missed Sutton.

*You just saw her last night.*

Too long ago. Now that they'd put the past behind them, they were becoming better together, easier, with fewer awkward moments in between. Sadly, there'd been no more kissing. Casey should ask her out on a date, preferably a dinner date, but lunch would work just as well. Why not now? He made the two-block trek to Sutton's office with a bounce in his step.

She was in a meeting. And had two more scheduled after that.

Feeling at loose ends, he returned to his office in Cargo Coffee and glared at the perpetually grinning Santa. "What are you so happy about?"

Plastic dude gave him a blank stare.

"Yeah, well, I don't like that look in your eye." He zeroed in on the wide girth. "You've been hitting the cookie jar a bit too hard. You could use some exercise, pal."

And Casey could use some practice towing the plastic ornament behind him. He pinged Reno. I'm heading to the mountain for a couple practice runs before the parade. You in?

Reno's one-word response came seconds later. Always.

Excellent. Pick you up in fifteen minutes.

It took Casey closer to twenty to change clothes

and answer Emory's endless questions about switching up the Christmas displays. "Do what you think is best. But," he added with a pointed look. "Don't go crazy."

"Gotcha."

He was nearly out the door, Santa tucked under his arm like a giant football, when she stopped him a second time, "Oh, Casey, one more thing."

Readjusting Santa, no easy task, he gave her his undivided attention. "Yeah?"

"I think we should start a raffle."

"What kind of raffle?"

She quickly outlined her idea. "Customers will fill out a small form with their name, phone number and email address, or they can toss in their business cards. Then, every Friday we'll draw one or two names. The winner, or winners, will receive enough coffee and bakery items to feed themselves and several of their closest friends."

Sounded expensive. "How many of their closest friends?"

"I don't know, maybe ten? And before you say no, think about this. We'd have all those lovely names and emails to send out promotional materials."

Still sounded expensive, but he liked the idea. "When would we start collecting these names and business cards?"

"Immediately."

"Yeah, okay." He dragged a hand through his hair. "Fine, do it."

She blinked. "I'm sorry, what was that?"

"I said, do it. Start a raffle."

"No pushback?" she asked. "No request for a cost analysis. No, 'let me think about it.' Or 'I'll get back to you on this'?"

"I'm feeling benevolent today." He nearly told her they could do something better than coffee and bakery items, but he wasn't sure what that something was. He had ideas, but nothing he wanted to mention until he'd run a…cost analysis.

"Problem?" he asked when Emory continued standing there, blinking at him.

"Not a single one. And watch this. Me scurrying away before you change your mind." She backpedaled toward the counter, picking up speed with each step.

"You can really move when you put your mind to it."

She laughed. Casey did, too. Mind still on raffles, he exited the building and tossed Santa in the back of his truck. When he pulled to a stop outside The Slippery Slope, Reno yanked open the passenger door with a snarl. "You're late."

"By six whole minutes."

"Yeah, well, six minutes of lost daylight is five and three-quarters too many."

And people called *him* Ebenezer Grinch. "What's got you in such a pleasant mood?"

"Not what," Reno ground out through gritted teeth. "Who."

"Want to toss out a name to go with that frown?" Casey offered in an oh-so-helpful voice.

"No, I want to get to the slopes and work off my temper," he said while absently rubbing his shoulder, the one he'd shattered in a career-ending crash. There'd been hard days of recovery after that, and some exceptionally low points, the lowest being an addiction to painkillers. But Reno had come out on the other end a better man.

Nevertheless, Casey didn't like the way his friend continued working the kinks out of his shoulder. "You okay to ski today?"

"I'm good."

"Said the man still massaging his bum shoulder."

"Knock it off, *Mom*."

Casey grinned, completely unoffended by Reno's insult. He *was* sounding like a parent and blamed it on time spent with Toby. A twinge of emotion wanted to move through him. Satisfaction? Pride? The love of a father for a son? He liked all three sensations.

"Are we doing this or not?"

"We're doing this." Casey put the truck in gear and headed to the base of the mountain.

While he searched for a parking spot, Reno glanced in the back of the truck, did a fast double take, then whistled low in his throat. "That has got to be the ugliest plastic Santa I have ever seen."

"You are not wrong."

He swung back around, eyebrows raised. "Where did Ugly St. Nick come from?"

"That, my friend, was a gift. Compliments of the mayor."

"Dude, Sutton must really dislike you."

The fact that she continued engaging in their Santa war said the opposite. Which reminded Casey of the idea for his next prank. He explained it to his friend.

Reno approved. "Classic."

The two of them—three if you counted Santa—made their way to the ski lift. At the top of the mountain, Reno turned all business. Casey took the other man's lead and got to work securing Santa to the sled he'd carted up with his other gear.

Clearly impatient to get started, Reno pulled his goggles into place, swished around a bit, then saluted Casey. "Meet you at the bottom."

Off he went, straight down the first fifty yards of the run, a bullet of red and blue careening down the mountain. Casey didn't even try to keep up. Towing a six-foot plastic Santa required a slow but steady approach. Not as easy as it sounded. Casey found his rhythm by the third run, and was holding his own with Reno by the fifth—well, if keeping the man in sight counted as *holding his own*.

Just to see what he was capable of, Casey tucked Santa and his sled in a secret spot for later, then tackled the mountain unencumbered. He came to a swooshing halt next to Reno at the bottom of the mountain. Out of breath but not out of dignity, he clapped his friend on the back. "You, my man, are still a beast on the slopes."

Reno curled his lip in self-disgust. "Compared to my former self, I'm a turtle."

Something in the other man's voice gave Casey pause. "You miss competing?"

"Like someone cut off a limb." Which had nearly happened, if not for the skill of the orthopedic surgeon who'd literally pieced Reno's shoulder back together.

"That's rough."

Reno gave a philosophical grunt. "My own fault. I knew the risks every time I took to the slopes. I ignored them. But, yeah, I knew what they were."

"Reno Miller taking personal accountability for his actions. You really are a new man."

"Not according to some people." He shook his head.

The comment begged for an explanation, but now that the sun had set, skiers were gathering for the parade, some solo, some in groups, families of adults and kids, some even younger than Toby. Casey really needed to get the boy on the mountain and show him the basics.

The idea of teaching the boy how to ski reminded Casey that he and Jeremy had tackled the bunny slopes together at the ripe old age of three. The thought brought back a slew of bittersweet memories and one huge regret. Jeremy should be the one teaching his son how to ski. But he couldn't, so Casey would do it for him. Maybe he'd even get Sutton on a pair of skis again. She'd been fierce back in the day. Her kid would be impressed.

As if thinking about the woman could make her appear, he spotted her moving through the crowd. Toby trotted alongside her, his mouth moving as fast as his feet. Shaking her head firmly, Sutton appeared to be telling the boy no to whatever he was asking her. Parenting, Casey was fast discovering, required a lot of headshaking. Holding firm, staying the course, never backing down unless there was a good reason.

Toby saw Casey and waved. Casey raised his hand in return. The next thing he knew, the boy was barreling in his direction and Sutton was the one hustling to keep pace with her son. But then she saw Casey and slowed her steps to a more reasonable trot.

He thought he detected a hint of amusement in her expression, and something that looked like affection. Directed solely at him. The responding tug in his heart felt intimate, familiar, like old times, but with a promise of bigger things to come.

Toby skidded to a stop just short of running into him. "Hey, Mr. Casey."

"Hey, buddy." He pulled the kid into a bear hug that had the kid laughing. "How was school today?"

"It was okay." Toby shrugged, the gesture reminding Casey of…himself. The boy was picking up his mannerisms. Terrifying to think he was being watched that closely by the little guy. What if he slipped up? The weight of responsibility nearly brought Casey to his knees.

"Are you going to watch the parade with me and Mom?"

"I'd love to, but I can't."

"How come?"

"Because I'll be skiing in the parade."

"Really?" Toby's eyes widened. "That's so cool."

It struck Casey, then. He'd actually, willingly signed up to carry flares in the Torchlight Parade. He hadn't been coerced, or dogged by the mayor, or bullied into it. He'd actually, *willingly* volunteered. When had he begun to participate in the town's Christmas events?

Right around the time Sutton bulldozed back into his life and brought her seven-year-old little boy with her.

The woman in question chose that moment to give Casey one of those long, searching stares of hers. He hated when she did that. It made his heart pound too hard and his head spin too fast. Once again, he couldn't look away, could barely think. He even had to suppress the urge to lean down and brush his lips across hers.

As if reading his intent, she gave him a slow, secretive grin. "Hey, there."

"Hey." And that display of witty banter was why women—this one in particular—never fell at his feet.

Sutton was so busy watching Casey watch her that she didn't notice Reno motioning her over until her son nudged her arm. "*Mom*, Mr. Reno wants something."

"Oh, yes, I see. Thanks, baby." She said a hasty goodbye and approached her friend. He was all by himself, a microphone in his hand, a frown on his face. That couldn't be good. "Where's Phoebe?" she asked.

His scowl deepened. "I was about to ask you the same thing."

*Really* not good. Sutton checked her phone, thumbed open her contacts page and scrolled down to the Ps. Just as she was typing out a text, one came through. "It's from Phoebe."

"And…?"

"She's running late." Sutton shoved her phone in her pocket.

"Why?"

"She didn't give an explanation. Can you begin without her?"

"Yeah, sure." Reno's voice lacked conviction. "I just have to give a few instructions to the skiers, hand out the flares, and we're good to go."

She studied his body language, which was all but vibrating with uncertainty. It was rare to see Reno Miller flustered. His lack of confidence filled her with the same emotion. She chased her gaze around the assembled skiers, stopping on Casey.

A silent message passed between them, and then he was on the move, tugging Toby with him. "What's up?" he asked.

Reno answered. "The parade coordinator is MIA."

"Not missing in action," Sutton corrected. "Running late."

Reno snorted. "Same difference."

This wasn't the time to argue semantics. Casey must have come to the same conclusion, because he said, "Don't worry, Sutton. I've got this."

He consulted with Reno for a few minutes, then nodded and shouldered his way through the crowd. Reno followed, then both men disappeared in the colorful sea of bobbing beanie caps. Casey popped back into view first. Climbing on top of a picnic table, he called for quiet.

A hush fell over the skiers.

Putting authority in his voice and using the kind of succinct language that must have served him well in the military, he gave the parade participants detailed instructions. The smile he produced as he spoke was new, or rather old. Casey looked like his old self, before his girlfriend had broken his heart. Maybe, by telling Sutton about Victoria, he'd let the hurt go and could now enjoy the season. Maybe it was his afternoons with Toby.

And maybe, just maybe, it was the time he'd spent with her.

Sutton reveled in the jolt of pleasure stealing through her. Until this moment, she hadn't allowed herself to believe that she and Casey could find their way back to each other. Oh, she'd known they were growing closer. Hadn't she said as much? But this new spark of hope gave her confidence that they could have a future together.

Smiling, Sutton took Toby's hand. "Let's find a good spot to watch the parade."

"Okay."

Hand in hand, they wove their way through the crowd forming at the base of the mountain. Toby looked up at the night sky. "How come we're having a parade at night?"

"It's easier to see the flares in the dark. You'll understand what I mean soon."

As if on cue, instrumental Christmas music erupted from outdoor speakers and the parade began. Skiers made the trek down the mountain in a zigzag pattern. One, then, two, then four, more and more, like ants marching in formation toward home. Within minutes, the mountain glowed with hundreds of flares. The effect was amazing, jaw-dropping, especially for a first timer like her son.

Just when Sutton thought the night couldn't get any more perfect, a light, fluffy snow began falling in big, fat, slow-moving flakes.

Toby sighed in little-boy awe. "Oh, Mom. This is so...cooooool."

"Very cool," she agreed, hoping—praying— the magazine judges were in the crowd watching the spectacle with equal wonder and awe.

The skiers kept coming. "Hey, look. There's Mr. Casey."

"Where? I don't see him."

"There. He's in the very back, next to Mr.

Reno, and behind that lady on the snowboard."
That lady, if Sutton wasn't mistaken, was Phoebe
Foxe. The sheriff's deputy had made it.

"Do you see him?" Toby asked. "Do you see
Mr. Casey?"

"I see him." Boy, did she ever. She'd forgotten
how good he looked on a pair of skis. Confident
and in control.

"Look, Mom. Look, look, look." Toby tugged
on her arm with one hand and pointed with the
other. "He's pulling something behind him."

Sutton narrowed her eyes, seeing what her son
saw but not quite processing the picture. As more
people joined in the pointing, and began whispering, snickering, Sutton blew out a long, steady
breath. She'd have to hand it to Casey. That was
one creative use of a sled.

Toby burst out laughing. "It's…" he could
hardly speak he was laughing so hard. "It's
*Santa*."

Yep. It was Santa all right, riding tall and proud
on a red sled.

Sutton wanted to be upset, but she'd started
this crazy battle of theirs. And the crowd seemed
to love the gag, as evidenced by their cheers and
comments. Some of which they directed to the
plastic decoration. "Hey, Santa, you get my letter
yet?" and "What, no coffee today?" and "How'd
the caroling go the other night?"

Somewhere along the way, the Santa war between Casey and Sutton had become a running joke that the entire town was in on.

"Hey, Mom. Can I go—"

"No, you cannot."

Toby's mouth fell open. "How can you say no? You don't even know what I was going to ask."

"Doesn't matter. The fireworks are about to start."

"Do you think Mr. Casey will watch them with us?"

The odds were not in their favor. He had a plastic Santa to deal with. He'd probably try to hide the old guy, unless she preempted the move. Out came her phone. The text was brief, but she trusted Maria to do her job.

Not long after putting her phone away, Sutton caught sight of Casey ambling in their direction. Toby called out to him. Waving, he picked up the pace. He was alone, no plastic Santa in sight, strolling toward them with his signature long, loose-limb strides. Snowflakes fell in lazy swirls around him. Some of the fat flakes landed in his thick black hair. A few found their resting place on his broad shoulders, while others joined their predecessors at his feet.

Sutton's heart squeezed at the sight of all that masculine confidence moving along without a care in the world, looking rather proud of himself. "Where's Santa?"

"I'll never tell."

He'd barely spoken the words when the first fireworks shot in the sky.

Sutton flinched at the loud boom, which was followed by another bang-bang-bang, then a screaming whistle. The noise was too much. Her head grew light, her shoulders swayed.

"Hey," Casey whispered, his arm going around her shoulders. "Listen with your eyes, not with your ears."

She laughed at the ridiculous suggestion. "You're such a dork."

"A really smart dork. Go on, give it a try."

The advice was absurd, and yet she found herself snuggling against him and turning her face to the sky. She never took her eyes off the shooting lights, not even as the booming, buzzing, hissing, crackling and humming filled the night air. Slowly, she relaxed.

"That's my girl."

Oh, yes. Yes, she was. And he was her guy.

Toby stood in front of them, leaning on Casey so he could crane his neck for a better view. The little boy laughed, sighed, and every time he commented on a particularly pretty firework, Casey told him what it was called. "Those are killer bees."

"I like them because they whistle."

"Me, too," he agreed.

"What's that one called?" Toby pointed to the burst of colorful stars.

"That's a peony. And that one on its right, that's a screaming spider. And that one—" Casey pointed to a firework that left a trail of silver stars cascading down like the branches of a weeping willow "—is a—can you guess?"

"A willow," Sutton said, smiling at the pretty picture in the sky.

"Correct."

The rest of the night went by in a happy blur. Smiling, and using the word *awesome* a lot, Toby kept up an ongoing Q&A session with Casey. Sutton leaned into the man and listened to his responses. The flicker of hope that had sparked in her heart earlier surged into a colorful burst of heat. This was the life she wanted. The life she could have. It was within her reach.

Her phone vibrated with an incoming text. With Casey distracted by Toby, she checked the screen. I've got Santa.

Yes. Her assistant had come through. Hunching over her phone, Sutton typed out a quick reply. Remind me to give you a raise.

Maria's heart emoji summed up the evening perfectly.

# *Chapter Fourteen*

Sutton all but floated through the next seven days, gliding along on the bliss she felt over her restored relationship with Casey and the deep sense of relief that every holiday event up to this point had gone smoothly. Although she was beyond pleased, not all of the events were a crashing success among those closest to her.

Toby hadn't been a fan of the Candlelight Tour of Homes, or as he groused, "Why do we have to walk around a bunch of old houses?" Casey had grumbled right along with the boy. "Yeah, and why are there so many of them?" Both man and boy had been much more enthusiastic about riding on the North Pole Express.

The next big event would make her son even happier. Proving her point, Toby all but bounced into the kitchen on the morning of the Soap Box Derby. "It's race day, Mom."

"I'm aware. You're going to have so much fun,

kiddo." Grabbing a bowl with one hand and a box of cereal with the other, she placed both in front of the boy. "Not only at the race, but later. We've got lots of events planned for the afternoon."

After much debate, Sutton and her staff had decided to hold the race at the Ice Castles. A calculated move that would show off Thunder Ridge's world-famous attraction to race spectators who might not otherwise make the trip up the mountain. Bonus, the 950-foot hill on the south end of the main parking lot met the All-American Soap Box Derby requirements, both in length and grade.

"Can we go now?"

"Not until you sit down and eat your breakfast."

"Okay." The boy shoveled cereal into his mouth at a speed just shy of Reno's world-record pace down the slopes.

As she watched her son mow through his breakfast, Sutton sipped her coffee and let her mind wander back to the night before. Casey had joined them for dinner before they'd headed out as a trio to hop on the North Pole Express. When they'd arrived home, an exhausted Toby insisted Casey tuck him into bed. The boy had fallen asleep halfway through his prayers.

Sutton had then walked Casey out to his car. He'd kissed her good-night, the moment lasting longer than the last time she'd found herself in his arms. Smiling at the memory, she touched her lips. Sighed a little. Smiled some more.

Toby glanced up from his bowl of cereal. "You say something, Mom?"

She dropped her hand. "I have a good feeling about the race."

"Me, too. I'm going to beat Samson. I've practiced a lot. Like more than a lot, and Mr. Casey says I'm ready."

"You've worked hard, Toby. I'm proud of you."

"Yeah? Even if I don't win?"

"Even if you don't win."

Her son's grin was so like his father's, all the way down to the dimple in his right cheek. The sorrow came again, but not as deep, or as painful. She would always love Jeremy, but it was time to let him go. *Goodbye, my friend.*

Twenty minutes after loading Toby into the back seat of her BMW, Sutton turned onto Casey's property. At the exact moment she shut off the ignition, her son exited the car. She followed him a second later and looked around. Casey was nowhere in sight, but her father and uncle were placing toolboxes and other gear in the flatbed of Horace's truck.

Toby rushed over to them. Sutton settled for a wave. The two men acknowledged her with identical nods. Horace and Beau may be family only by marriage, but they'd remained close long after Sutton's mother had run off. *The family we choose*, she thought, pleased that both men were in her son's life. And hers.

Casey appeared on his front porch dressed in battered jeans, a light blue Henley shirt and his leather bomber jacket. The man could look better, but it was hard to imagine how. He still hadn't decorated his house beyond the two strings of lights. Instead of upsetting Sutton, the picture of him standing beneath those sad little lights tugged at her heart. Not with sympathy or pity, but with scorn for the woman who'd hurt him so badly he'd sworn off Christmas.

Her heart was too full to end on that negative thought. She lifted her hand in greeting. He immediately went on the move. He stopped in front of her and gave her that smile that slid right into her heart and squeezed.

"Big day," she said, surprised her voice sounded so steady with her head spinning out of control.

"Oh, yeah. Really big day."

In that moment, Sutton realized the truth that had been in her heart all along. She loved Casey. She loved him with a fierceness that was richer, deeper, stronger than before. And she needed some air or else she'd be blubbering all over him. Going for a smooth exit, she glanced at her watch.

"Wow, is that the time? I gotta get going. Lots of preparations yet."

Casey's smile softened and his eyes crinkled at the corners. "Don't you have a small army to handle the pesky details?"

"An army is only as strong as its general."

"When you put it that way…" He snapped to attention and saluted her. "Carry on, ma'am."

Sutton managed to say goodbye and climb into her car. But her mind raced. How had she let this happen? How had she fallen in love with Casey all over again?

Because she'd never fully fallen out of love with him.

What did that say about her marriage? Her feelings for Jeremy had been real, she assured herself, built on a solid foundation of friendship. That had been enough for Sutton. Had it been enough for her husband? The question nagged her all the way up the mountain and into the parking lot.

She sat a moment, digesting her thoughts. Truth be told, her marriage to Jeremy had been no great romance for either of them. She'd had her work, and he'd had his. They'd been happy, though, and had made a perfect little boy together. For that blessing alone, Jeremy would always have a place in her heart.

Feeling better, she stepped into the sounds and smells of a small county fair. Almost immediately, she caught sight of Casey's brother McCoy, the mastermind behind the Ice Castles and the man in charge of the Soap Box Derby. She called out his name.

He crooked a finger to call her over where he stood beside the racetrack.

"Ready for today?" she asked.

"More than ready."

"Good answer." Hand shielding her eyes, she studied the track's setup. The ramp stood on her right, the finish line on her left. Two distinct lanes were separated by orange cones. Shortened hay bales had also been stacked on the outer edges. Tents for the participants and their pit crews were filling up fast with contestants. "Looks like you have everything well in hand."

"We do."

"Then I won't get in your way." She'd made it two full steps before a voice from one of the food vendor tents called out to her. "Mayor Wentworth, can I have a moment of your time?"

"Of course." She answered the man's questions, fielded several more from other vendors.

Excitement hung in the air.

By the time Sutton found Toby's tent at the end of the course, the boy was hanging on Casey's every word, while her father and uncle buzzed around the car.

There were four other members of Toby's pit

crew, three of them of the canine variety. Casey had dressed his bulldogs in Christmas sweaters. Winston sported reindeer antlers, which made her laugh. But it was the final crew member that had her reaching for her phone and sending her assistant a job-well-done text. Maria had followed Sutton's instructions to the letter. Santa wore grease-stained coveralls with a wrench taped to one of his hands and a paintbrush to the other.

After high-stepping over the hay bales serving as barricades, Sutton ducked under the tent, turned her phone sideways and started clicking pictures from the camera app. "Say cheese," she told Santa.

Thinking she meant him, Toby ran over, slung his arm around the thick plastic waist, and yelled, "Cheeeese."

Sutton laughed.

"Everyone, quickly now, gather around for a group shot."

There was a moment of chaos as the team scrambled into place. Casey stood behind Toby, one hand on the boy's shoulder, Louie in the other. Sutton's father and uncle moved into the flank positions. Winston and Clementine settled at their feet.

"Perfect." She took several photos, then several more. "Got it."

The group separated. Casey set the puppy back

on the ground, then said to Toby, "Let's show your mom your technique." He set a helmet on the boy's head, adjusted the strap, then directed him to climb into the car. "Okay, little man, what's first?"

"This." Hunching low in his seat, Toby leaned forward.

"Where do your feet go?"

"Here."

Casey looked inside the car. "That's right."

"Now your hands."

Sutton couldn't see what her son was doing with his hands, but he was very focused, as was Casey. "A little higher, there. That's it. You're a pro already."

Smiling, Casey looked over his shoulder and winked at Sutton. Words deserted her. Thoughts scattered. She was back to another time, watching Casey prepare for his first race. Her eyes burned.

"Hey, Sutton." Casey straightened. "You okay?"

"I…" She smiled. "Excellent. Never better." A stellar acting job on her part. Hollywood would be calling any moment.

Casey strolled over. "I have sisters. I know when a woman is on the verge of crying."

"I'm thinking how lovely it is to see Toby so happy. I know I've said this before, but it bears repeating. Thank you, Casey."

"This was a team effort," he said, shrugging

his shoulder in a gesture her son had picked up. "Toby did most of the heavy lifting. But your father and uncle were invaluable, as well."

Sutton blinked back more tears. She'd been the one to restore the derby, but Casey had been the one to turn it into a family affair. "Thank you," she whispered again.

"Don't thank me yet. Next year, you're getting your hands dirty."

"Count on it."

A voice came over the loudspeaker calling for the racers and one representative from each team to the officials' tent for final instructions. "Come on, Toby. That's us."

He helped the boy out of the car and the two of them joined the queue of participants filing toward the official race tent.

The rest of the morning was a long, entertaining, series of action-packed races. Sutton cheered with the rest of the spectators, but twice as hard when it was Toby's turn to speed down the track. The competition in each division consisted of three timed intervals, two cars in each lane, one per heat. The car and driver that achieved the fastest single run would be declared the winner. That proved to be Toby, with Samson coming in a close second.

At the awards ceremony, the two boys stood arm in arm, holding up their individual trophies and grinning wildly. As Sutton took pictures with her phone, she was reminded of Casey and Jeremy, not much older than her son, holding up their trophies.

"Oh, Casey, isn't it amazing?" She took more pictures, then lowered her phone and smiled at the man standing beside her. "Toby took first place."

"That was the plan." His eyes full of nostalgia, he took her hand. For several beats, his gaze held hers, intensely now. "I'm honored you trusted me enough to guide your son through the process."

The way he was looking at her, it stole her breath. "I'm glad it was you, Casey." She lifted up and brushed her mouth to his. "Really glad."

"I dare you to do that again, later, when we don't have an audience." He gave a slight nod to where her father and uncle stood. "And now, here comes our winner." He nodded again, this time to the little boy sprinting in their direction.

"Mom! Mom! Look what I won!" Toby proudly presented the trophy that was nearly as tall as he was. "And all I had to do was work hard and steer straight."

Sutton laughed. "Valuable life lessons."

"That's what Mr. Casey said." He grinned up at the man. "Isn't that right?"

"I seem to remember saying something like that."

Toby touched the trophy, then did a little wiggle. "This is one of the best days of my life."

Sutton's sentiments exactly.

Still holding Sutton's hand, Casey watched Toby's impromptu celebration with a lump in his throat. It was hard not to think of Jeremy while his son danced around with the same atrocious lack of rhythm. Jeremy had been good at many things. Dancing was not one of them.

Casey grinned as the kid nearly tripped over his own two feet. He'd felt his friend's presence all day, more now that the races were over, and the trophies were being handed out. He and Jeremy had stood in the winner's circle every year they'd competed.

For Casey, the Soap Box Derby had been about friendship. His and Jeremy's. Today, it was about family. Jeremy's family, the one he'd put second to his career. Casey had a good idea why his friend had been so driven. But to confirm his suspicions would require asking Sutton more questions. Casey couldn't take the risk.

He could, however, enjoy watching her celebrate with her son. He let go of her hand so she could join in the happy dance. The way she smiled at Toby did something strange to Casey's insides. A stronghold of banked emotions struggled to break free. He wanted Sutton back in his life, permanently. He'd liked to think they were on the right path to make that happen and that they'd put the past behind them. But he feared it was only on a temporary hold.

Sutton was too smart for her own good. She was already looking at the night of her eighteenth birthday with that sharp brain of hers. She'd already guessed that Casey had been protecting a friend. How long would it be before she figured out which friend?

It was a relief when his brother motioned him from the other side of the tent. "Looks like McCoy needs me. Be right back."

"We'll be here."

McCoy handed him a phone. "Reno wants to talk to you."

"Why didn't he call me on my cell?"

"I don't know. Ask him yourself."

Casey put the phone to his ear and listened to his friend's very interesting intel. "Describe them," he demanded, looking around while Reno said, "One is a tall guy, older, full beard, lots of shaggy gray hair, black wool coat, no hat."

"Got him," Casey said. "He's with two women, one nearly as tall as he, wearing a nondescript beige coat."

"Is the other woman wearing one of those multicolored winter caps with the long straps that look like pigtails?"

Casey considered the hat in question. "Yep."

"You, my friend, are looking at the judges from the travel magazine."

Trying not to stare, he hissed out a breath. "How do you know?"

"I cannot reveal my source."

Of course, Reno would be difficult. "You're certain they're the judges?" Casey asked. "Absolutely sure?"

"I'd stake The Slippery Slope on it."

Okay, then.

"But wait," Reno said. "There's more." Casey listened to the rest of his friend's revelation. When he finally disconnected the call and handed the phone back to McCoy, he wasn't sure what to do about what he'd just heard.

His brother eyed him closely. "Are you going to tell Sutton?"

"Don't know yet. I need to think." This wasn't the kind of information he could tell Sutton and then expect her to unhear it once he had. Then again, keeping secrets from her hadn't worked well for either of them.

Bottom line, there would be unfortunate ramifications no matter what decision he made. Casey's feet carried him through the tent, away from Sutton and Toby, then back again when he saw the boy run off toward his friend.

"Sutton, I need to tell you something. But not here. Take a walk with me."

She must have seen something in his face because she did as he asked without argument. Her eyes, a confused blue, skimmed over him as he drew her to a stop at the end of the now deserted racetrack. "What's wrong, Casey?"

"I know the identity of the judges."

"You…how?"

"A friend of a friend told me." Not completely inaccurate. "All three of the judges are here today, standing right over there in the tent we just left. Want me to point them out to you?"

"Absolutely not." She looked as horrified as she sounded.

"So that's a no?"

"Of course it's a no. Casey, I would never be able to pass them on the street without smiling at them, or trying to figure out how to sway them without letting them know I know who they are. I…no." She raised her hands in the universal show of surrender. "I can't be trusted with that information."

He laughed. "Do you want to know what else I heard?"

She answered without hesitation. "No. Yes. No. Maybe." She shook her head. "I don't know. Is it…?" She glanced to her right, then her left, then right again. "Is it bad?"

"It's not great. Thunder Ridge is in the lead, but just barely."

"What?" She looked seriously appalled. "How are we not blowing Village Green out of the water?"

"It has something to do with some sort of flash mob that they put on yesterday."

"A flash mob? Seriously?" She rolled her eyes. "How lame."

"The judges really liked it. Apparently, the clever Christmas medley included singers, instruments, the entire high school marching band, two movie stars who winter in Village Green, and some big-name rock star."

"Oh. Wow." She sighed. "How do we beat that?"

"I have an idea."

He explained about the raffle already underway at Cargo Coffee. "But instead of giving away coffee and bakery items, I'll take the winners up in the air at night. Thunder Ridge makes a really great impression from the sky."

Sutton's gaze never faltered from his face. "There's a serious flaw in your plan. You can't guarantee the magazine judges will enter the raffle. And even if they do, how would you choose their names without cheating someone else out of the chance to take the flight?"

She was right. He thought a moment, came up

with a solution that wouldn't involve the raffle at all. "I have a better idea. I would—"

"No, Casey. There's no way you can pull this off without crossing a line. It's just not possible. And besides, weren't you the one who said Thunder Ridge has to win on a level playing field or not at all?"

He was almost insulted. "Give me a little credit, Sutton. I have no intention of playing favorites."

"Oh, really? The fact that you know who the judges are is already an advantage, and that leads me to think you're up to your old tricks."

Now he *was* insulted. "Old tricks? What are you accusing me of, Sutton?"

"All right, here it is. I think you're planning to do something bad with that raffle, for the sake of something good. And that, I won't allow."

"You think I would cheat?"

"I didn't say that."

"Yeah, you did." He turned to pace and, running a hand through his hair, put some much-needed distance between them. Over his shoulder, he pinned her with a sharp stare. "You still don't trust me. No matter what I say or do, you immediately jump to the conclusion that my motives are shady. You just can't give me the benefit of the doubt, can you, Sutton?"

She didn't deny it. Instead, she pointed a finger

at him. "You do this, Casey, and try to pull off a win for Thunder Ridge without my approval, and you and I are going to have a problem."

They'd come so far, in just three short weeks, only to find themselves right back at the beginning. "Is that a threat?"

"It's a promise."

"Then we have a problem."

# Chapter Fifteen

Sutton stood alone on the tarmac, her gaze locked on the sleek airplane making its final approach into the Thunder Ridge Regional Airport. She fought to stay calm, to keep panic from sending her logic into a tailspin. No easy feat. Her mind was a tangle of conflicting thoughts and emotions.

Despite his assertion three days ago, Sutton trusted Casey, she really did. She knew his character. Knew he would never intentionally sabotage Thunder Ridge's chances of winning the contest. But she also knew he'd gone against her wishes and taken the magazine judges up in the air on a late-night flight.

The plane touched down in a smooth, picture-perfect landing.

Sutton waited as the aircraft taxied down the runway, came to a stop outside the hangar and powered down. She continued waiting as the door came open, a small stepladder descended, and the passengers began disembarking. Two women, an elderly gentleman and, lastly, Casey himself wearing his signature bomber jacket and ball cap.

Even in her frustration, the sight of him had Sutton's heart slamming against her ribs. Stupid heart. She fisted her gloved hands, resisting the urge to march up to him and demand an explanation for his duplicity. Not yet. Not in front of the judges who were drawing together in a small huddle, comparing notes from the tiny books in their hands.

A small sound of dismay slipped past her lips.

Casey snapped his head in her direction. A muscle shifted at his jaw, then he was smiling broadly and offering his hand to each of the three people who'd exited the plane ahead of him. He shook the women's first. "Thank you, Fiona, Mavis," he said, then turned to the man, "Charles. It was an honor showing off our small piece of Colorado."

The smaller of the two women spoke for the group. "It's us who should be thanking you, Mr. Evans. You've given us a broad spectrum of clarity."

"Glad to hear it."

Sutton tried not to gape. The judges appeared pleased, not just with their recent flight but with

Casey himself. A vague sense of doubt wanted to test her brain and move into her heart.

Casey began speaking again. "Give me five minutes to secure my plane and I'll drive you back into town."

"No need. Our ride is here." Fiona Masterson, the head judge, pointed to Sutton, smiled. "Evening, Mayor."

"Evening, Fiona."

"Ah." Without missing a beat, Casey said polite goodbyes to each of the judges, thanked them again for their time, then turned back to his plane.

Picking up where he left off, Sutton said, "Let's get you three out of the cold." She directed them to her car. While they were getting settled, she asked them to give her a minute.

She trotted over to Casey. "I need a word."

He studied her from beneath the bill of his ball cap. "Now is not a good time."

"Please."

He paused, dropped another unreadable gaze over her. "Where's Toby?"

"At my father's."

He said, "Okay," but not in a way that sounded like anything was okay.

"Are you going to tell me what's going on here, Casey? And why you thought it was a good idea to go against my wishes?"

"What if I told you I flew the judges over both Thunder Ridge and Village Green?"

She nearly laughed, but it caught in her throat. "Doesn't change the fact that no one was supposed to know their identities."

He took off the ball cap, ran his hand over his head in a gesture of frustration. "I didn't seek out their identities, Sutton. It was relayed to me by a man who'd already told my brother, and no telling who else. Like, oh, say…you? And while we're on the subject, how come you and Fiona are on a first-name basis?"

"Damage control."

"What do you think this entire night was about, if not damage control on my part?"

"Oh, really?"

"Yes, really. If I was able to find out who the judges were, others could, as well. Including people in Village Green."

True. But still. "I asked you not to do this."

"And I asked you to trust me."

His words echoed in her brain, bringing them back to the beginning of their troubles. To a place neither could seem to get past. "I tried."

"Not good enough, Sutton. Not if we're going to have a future together. Either you're all in, or not at all."

The reflex to defend herself came fast. She could feel Casey's frustration, his hurt. She could also feel the moment he shut her out. The pain was real, nearly obscene, like sharp, burning icicles stabbing into her heart. There was nothing left to do but leave the scene before he walked away first. "Goodbye, Casey."

"So long, Sutton."

Her limbs were heavy with the sense of loss as she climbed into her car. She'd barely settled in when Fiona patted her hand in a very motherly fashion. "Don't be too hard on him, Mayor Wentworth. He's made a remarkable transformation in a few short weeks."

Of all the things she'd expected to come out of the woman's mouth, that did not make the top-ten list. Pun intended.

Fiona twisted around and smiled at her cohorts in the back seat. "Should I tell her?"

"Might as well," said the man, grinning into the rearview mirror.

Fiona settled back in her seat. "Can you keep a secret, Mayor?"

An odd sensation—part confusion, part anticipation—spread through her. "Of course."

"Although the announcement isn't for a few days, and I can't give you the official word yet, I can tell you that Thunder Ridge is exactly the kind of town that belongs on our list of top-ten Christmas destinations in the US."

Sutton's hands trembled on the steering wheel. "Are you saying…we won?"

"What I'm saying is that if a man like Ebenezer Grinch can go from refusing to decorate his coffee shop to attending every single Christmas event in town, it stands to reason a trio of magazine judges would want to know the man's story."

Sutton could feel warmth creeping into her cheeks. There were too many revelations to know which one to address first. She went with the most obvious one. "You know about Casey's nickname?"

"That and more. He's an honest man, and a fair one. He went out of his way to show off his hometown, and did the same for the competition."

"But…your identities were supposed to be secret."

"Some secret," came a masculine voice from the back seat. "Village Green found out about us on day one. They have yet to reveal this information. But oh, yeah. They know."

Sutton blinked at that startling revelation. "While that comes as a shock, that doesn't erase what Casey did. He took you up in the air under false pretenses."

"Now that's where you're mistaken. Mr. Evans was completely transparent from the moment he approached us with his offer. In fact, like you—" she looked pointedly at Sutton "—he not only told us how he knew our identities, but he let us know how and when he found out. His honesty, as well as yours, tells me the Christmas spirit is strong in Thunder Ridge."

"I...don't know what to say."

"You don't have to say anything. But if I were you..." she winked "...I'd be preparing my acceptance speech for when we announce the winner of our contest on Christmas Eve."

"Oh. Oh, my."

Mind spinning, Sutton dropped off the judges at their hotel. She sat in her car, thinking about past mistakes and transformations and trust. She owed Casey an apology, maybe even two. She would know exactly how many after she spoke with her uncle. He answered the door in his pajamas. "Did I wake you?"

"Not at all. Come in, come in." He stepped aside to let her pass. "I was debating between watching a Christmas movie or getting myself a snack. I decided on both."

She laughed. "Then I won't keep you long."

He directed her to follow him into his tiny kitchenette.

She sat, drumming her fingers on the chipped Formica.

"What's on your mind, Sutton?"

She was suddenly afraid. Afraid if her suspicions were right she would have to admit that everything she knew about herself, Jeremy, and their marriage was false. *Not everything.* Only a very small part. "I know Casey was covering for someone the night you arrested him."

"He told you that?"

She shook her head. "I figured it out on my own."

"I see."

"Did Casey ever tell you who he was protecting?"

"No, but I knew there was more going on than those boys were telling me."

*"Boys?"* Sutton sat up straighter. "I thought you only arrested Casey."

"I hauled in the other one, too."

"When you say the other one, you mean… Jeremy?"

Her uncle didn't answer her directly. "Think back to that night, Sutton. Review the details with that lawyer brain of yours, not with the emotions of a teenager."

"I'm trying."

Horace laid a hand on her arm, looked intently into her eyes, as if willing her to see the truth she'd blocked from her mind. "Who had the most to lose? Casey or Jeremy? One was still seventeen, the other eighteen. Which of the two confessed, and which one stayed silent?"

Suddenly, the pieces fell into place. Jeremy had

just turned eighteen. His record had to remain clean or the Air Force Academy would have revoked his appointment.

More memories came at her. The way Jeremy defended Casey that night, the next day, all the years after. She jumped to her feet. "I have to go."

He escorted her to the door. "Tell Casey I said hello."

Casey let the dogs out as soon as he arrived home from the airstrip. His jaw tight, he took a seat on the porch steps and watched the three animals play in the snow.

Their antics barely registered in his mind. He was too lost in thought. He couldn't stop thinking about Sutton and what might have been. They'd nearly made it this time. Had nearly put the past behind them. But something in Sutton couldn't give Casey the benefit of the doubt. And something in him couldn't stick around long enough to give her a chance to try.

What a sad, miserable pair they made.

His chest heaved with the weight of his sorrow. Louie dropped a squeaky ball at his feet. He threw it just as a faint hum in the distance had him looking up. Sutton's car pulled onto his property. Casey called out to the dogs to "play dead."

All three dropped to their haunches, staying put until he released them once Sutton's car came to a halt. He stared dully as she climbed out from the driver's seat and bent over to greet the animals one by one. She gave special attention to the puppy, wrestling the ball free from his mouth, then tossing it in a wide arc.

She made the trip to Casey next, lowered herself to the step beside him. "I owe you an apology. Actually, I owe you two. One for earlier and one for the night of my birthday party."

His breath jammed in his throat. It wasn't the words that got to him, it was the regret in them. The reflex to comfort her came fast and strong, too powerful to deny. He denied it anyway. "All right," he said. "I'm listening."

She gave him a small, wry smile. "I haven't shown you enough trust, not in the past or now. For that I am truly sorry."

Her words released a storm of emotion. "I'm sorry, too, Sutton. I haven't made it easy for you to trust me," he admitted, baring his soul in a way he'd never done before. "I pushed you away when things got rocky."

"And I let you." She dropped her head, lifted it again. "What is wrong with us? When we needed each other most, we let the other down."

"We made mistakes." He brushed a hand down her arm, casual and intimate, needing to touch her. "So now we can either continue letting them stand between us or start fresh."

"I like the idea of a new beginning."

He did, too. So why wasn't he reaching for her? Why wasn't she moving into his arms? Because Jeremy still stood between them, and maybe always would. "There are reasons why I shut you out, Sutton. Reasons I will never disclose."

"I know."

Something there, in her eyes. Forgiveness, understanding. Knowledge. "What is it you think you know?"

Her gaze turned tender, if a little sad. "Jeremy brought the beer. By covering for him you saved his appointment to the Air Force Academy. Oh, Casey." She took his hand, pulled it to her cheek, sighed deeply. "I've been so blind. The truth was there all along. I just had to look."

Her words produced a spark of hope. Such a wonderful, frightening sensation that stole his ability to respond.

"I never fully understood why Jeremy's career was so important to him. I get it now. He wanted to prove himself. Either as penance for his silence, or a way to honor the sacrifice you made for him." She kissed the palm of his hand, then let it go. "We'll never know his true motivation."

"I guess we won't." It was as close to an admission as he was going to give her. She didn't press for more, which took that sliver of hope in his heart and turned it into a blazing fire.

Her next words annihilated him. "I love you, Casey Evans. With all my heart, mind and soul. I'll stand by you, through the good and the bad. I will always trust. Until the day I die."

He wrapped his arm around her shoulders and pulled her close. "I love you, too, Sutton. With all my heart. I'll stay put through the good and the bad, until I take my very last breath."

"If that's how you truly feel, then why aren't you kissing me right now?"

He laughed, a short gruff sound deep in his throat. "I love you, Sutton Fowler Wentworth." He lowered his head, then paused to whisper, "To borrow a phrase from my favorite person, prepare to be amazed."

The words backfired on him. It was Casey who was amazed, by Sutton. Her kiss. Her generosity. Her presence in his life.

When he finally pulled away, she leaned her head back and stared up at the porch ceiling. "Now, about that pitiful strand of lights hanging from your roofline..."

# *Epilogue*

Christmas Eve was a busy day at City Hall. Lots to do before the travel magazine's official announcement at 7 p.m. sharp. Sutton and Casey exchanged a series of back-and-forth texts, but weren't able to meet in person due to her hectic schedule and his puzzling message: I'm working on something special for you and Toby.

Now, as she stood beside her son in the town square with the rest of Thunder Ridge, she patted her pocket where she'd tucked away her acceptance speech. She would keep her words brief. Winning, after all, was its own reward. Oh, who was she kidding. If it were up to her she'd talk for hours, maybe even gloat a little. But that would be poor form, so no. She would be succinct and gracious. Then she would celebrate with her two favorite guys.

"Hey, Mom. Where's Mr. Casey?"

Sutton looked around. "I don't know, baby. I'm sure he's here somewhere."

"He said he was coming, right?"

"That's what he said." He was also supposed to bring Toby's Christmas present with him, a little bulldog puppy named Louie. Casey would do the honors of giving her son the gift while Sutton took pictures with her phone.

So where was he?

As Fiona Masterson took the stage, a hush fell over the crowd. She began her speech with a thank-you to the residents of Thunder Ridge. Then she introduced the woman beside her. "This is Mavis Wallace. Our other colleague is in Village Green giving their mayor the news."

Interesting choice of words that had Sutton buzzing with anticipation. Fiona went on to say how much she enjoyed the Christmas season in both towns. Finally, she got to the point. "And the winner is..."

Sutton held her breath.

"Thunder Ridge, Colorado."

Cheers rang out, Toby's loudest of all. "Mom, we won!" He jumped up and down. "We won! We won! We won!"

And Casey had missed the announcement. Sutton trusted whatever had kept him away had been really important. As promised, she kept her speech brief. She was walking off the stage, wondering why Casey was *still* absent, when her phone vibrated with an incoming text. Come to my house, now. Bring the boy. Or it's curtains for Santa.

A picture followed and Sutton burst out laughing. Casey had tied acres of rope around the plastic Santa. There was only one proper response to such shenanigans. On our way.

Outside Casey's house, Sutton and Toby stood frozen in shock and wonder. Toby spoke first. "Wow."

Wow, indeed. There were so many multicolored lights Sutton considered shielding her son's eyes to prevent permanent damage. And that was only the beginning of the amazing spectacle. A massive Christmas wreath hung on the front door. Garland wrapped around the porch rails and columns. There were lawn ornaments, wire-framed reindeer and a Santa sleigh minus one very tacky plastic Santa.

Casey was also missing.

The front door swung open and there he stood framed in the doorway, wearing a red Christmas sweater and a smile so warm Sutton's insides ached with love.

"Mr. Casey!" Toby bounded up the steps ahead of Sutton.

The interior of the house was even more spectacular, the crowning glory a ten-foot tree covered in twinkling white lights and bright Christmas ornaments.

Still no sign of Santa.

Or little Louie, for that matter. Winston and Clementine, however, sprinted over to Toby with simultaneous barks. While the boy greeted the dogs, Casey relieved Sutton of her purse. Testing the weight, he frowned. "What's in this thing?"

"Only the essentials."

"Ah. Anyway..." He pulled Sutton into his arms. "Hey, beautiful."

"What are you doing?" she huffed out, laughing breathlessly.

"I'm kissing you."

"Oh, well, that's fine, then."

Toby looked up from the dogs and made a gagging sound. "Ugh, Mr. Casey, are you going to kiss my mom like that all the time?"

"A minimum of seven times each day, twice more on holidays and special occasions."

"Okay." Grinning, the little boy went back to playing with the dogs.

"Where's Louie," Sutton whispered into Casey's ear.

"Ready for his big moment. Be right back." He returned with a very handsome puppy sporting a red bow around his neck and a happy bulldog grin.

"Hey, Toby," Sutton said, "Come check out your Christmas present from Mr. Casey."

"What is it?" His eyes locked on Louie. "Oh...

Oh! He's mine? He's really, really mine? Like all mine?"

"He's all yours."

The boy's shriek of delight had all three dogs barking and Sutton taking photos on her phone. Casey passed the puppy into Toby's waiting arms. "Merry Christmas, Toby."

"Oh, thank you. Thank you, Mr. Casey!"

The puppy playfest and photo shoot lasted long enough for Casey to disappear and reappear with a very subdued plastic Santa. "You gagged him?" Sutton asked in mock horror.

"He got mouthy. I had to do something to shut him up."

They were laughing when Toby looked up and frowned. "What did you do to Santa." His eyes narrowed. "And, hey, what's that shiny thing hanging from his hand?"

"That, little man, is not for you. It's for your mom." Casey produced his most boyish grin. "Assuming she says yes."

Sutton's eyes filled as they locked on the diamond ring. She needed to add levity to the moment or she would turn into a crying, blubbering mess. "Is…" She brushed at her cheeks. "Is Santa asking me to marry him?"

"No, I am." Casey unhooked the ring and went down on one knee. "What you do say, Sutton? Will you marry me?"

"Say yes, Mom."

She reached out, pulled her hand back, sighed heavily. "I… Oh, Casey, I love you."

"I love you, too, but that's not an answer."

"Yes." She shot out her left hand. "Yes, I'll marry you."

He rose to his feet, slid the ring onto her finger, then pulled her back into his arms. "And that, Toby, is how it's done." Smiling, he stretched out his arm in silent invitation. "Come on, kiddo, get over here."

The little boy launched himself into their group hug and said, "Best Christmas ever."

Much later, with Toby asleep in his bed and the puppy curled up beside him, Sutton walked into Casey's arms and repeated her son's declaration. "Best Christmas ever."

\* \* \* \* \*

*If you loved this story,*
*check out the previous books*
*in the Thunder Ridge series by Renee Ryan*

Surprise Christmas Family
The Sheriff's Promise

*Available now from Love Inspired!*

*Find more great reads at*
*www.LoveInspired.com*

Dear Reader,

Christmas has always been my favorite holiday. I adore so much about the season. The decorations, the music, gathering with friends and family. I also love a good Christmas romance, the sappier the better, with the requisite happy ending. Add in puppies and sweet little boys and I'm a goner.

Christmas is also a time when friends and family come together to forgive old wounds. Sutton and Casey certainly had their share of past hurts to overcome. When I started writing this book, I never expected I would ultimately explore how our choices can leave lasting consequences. And how a promise made for all the right reasons could harm so many people. How easy it would have been for Casey to break his word to his friend and heal his relationship with Sutton. All it would have taken was a single conversation. But at what cost to his character?

In the end, he kept his friend's secret, even after the man's death, which presented a different dilemma for Sutton. She had to trust her instincts that he was the man she saw, not the man she remembered. She had to look beyond a single act to recognize Casey's true character.

I'm pleased I was able to give these two wounded souls a happy ending. I adored them, Santa pranks and all. I hope you enjoyed this book as much I did writing it. I love hearing from readers. Feel free to contact me at www.reneeryan.com. I'm also on Facebook. My Twitter handle is @reneeryanbooks.

Happy Reading,
*Renee.*

# Get 4 FREE REWARDS!

## We'll send you 2 FREE Books plus 2 FREE Mystery Gifts.

**Love Inspired** books feature uplifting stories where faith helps guide you through life's challenges and discover the promise of a new beginning.

FREE
Value Over
$20

---

**YES!** Please send me 2 FREE Love Inspired Romance novels and my 2 FREE mystery gifts (gifts are worth about $10 retail). After receiving them, if I don't wish to receive any more books, I can return the shipping statement marked "cancel." If I don't cancel, I will receive 6 brand-new novels every month and be billed just $5.24 each for the regular-print edition or $5.99 each for the larger-print edition in the U.S., or $5.74 each for the regular-print edition or $6.24 each for the larger-print edition in Canada. That's a savings of at least 13% off the cover price. It's quite a bargain! Shipping and handling is just 50¢ per book in the U.S. and $1.25 per book in Canada.* I understand that accepting the 2 free books and gifts places me under no obligation to buy anything. I can always return a shipment and cancel at any time. The free books and gifts are mine to keep no matter what I decide.

Choose one: ☐ **Love Inspired Romance Regular-Print** (105/305 IDN GNWC)      ☐ **Love Inspired Romance Larger-Print** (122/322 IDN GNWC)

Name (please print)

Address                                                                Apt. #

City                          State/Province                      Zip/Postal Code

**Email:** Please check this box ☐ if you would like to receive newsletters and promotional emails from Harlequin Enterprises ULC and its affiliates. You can unsubscribe anytime.

# Get 4 FREE REWARDS!

## We'll send you 2 FREE Books <u>plus</u> 2 FREE Mystery Gifts.

**Harlequin Heartwarming Larger-Print** books will connect you to uplifting stories where the bonds of friendship, family and community unite.

FREE Value Over $20

---

**YES!** Please send me 2 FREE Harlequin Heartwarming Larger-Print novels and my 2 FREE mystery gifts (gifts worth about $10 retail). After receiving them, if I don't wish to receive any more books, I can return the shipping statement marked "cancel." If I don't cancel, I will receive 4 brand-new larger-print novels every month and be billed just $5.74 per book in the U.S. or $6.24 per book in Canada. That's a savings of at least 21% off the cover price. It's quite a bargain! Shipping and handling is just 50¢ per book in the U.S. and $1.25 per book in Canada.* I understand that accepting the 2 free books and gifts places me under no obligation to buy anything. I can always return a shipment and cancel at any time. The free books and gifts are mine to keep no matter what I decide.

161/361 HDN GNPZ

Name (please print)

Address                                                                          Apt. #

City                                    State/Province                    Zip/Postal Code

**Email:** Please check this box ☐ if you would like to receive newsletters and promotional emails from Harlequin Enterprises ULC and its affiliates. You can unsubscribe anytime.

### Mail to the **Harlequin Reader Service:**
**IN U.S.A.:** P.O. Box 1341, Buffalo, NY 14240-8531
**IN CANADA:** P.O. Box 603, Fort Erie, Ontario L2A 5X3

Want to try 2 free books from another series! Call 1-800-873-8635 or visit www.ReaderService.com.

---

## COMING NEXT MONTH FROM
## Love Inspired

### NURSING HER AMISH NEIGHBOR
*Brides of Lost Creek* • by Marta Perry
Seeking a break from her nursing duties, Miriam Stoltzfus returns to Lost Creek
only to be met with her most difficult patient yet—her childhood neighbor,
Matthew King. While he's crushed in spirit after being injured in the accident
that killed his brother, can she heal his physical wounds *and* his heart?

### BLENDED AMISH BLESSINGS
*Redemption's Amish Legacies* • by Patricia Johns
When widower Paul Ebersole's kitten causes havoc in Haddie Petersheim's
creamery, they agree to repair the store together. Soon they realize they
have much in common. Supporting each other with their families might
bring them closer than they ever imagined...

### THEIR UNBREAKABLE BOND
*Rocky Mountain Family* • by Deb Kastner
Training avalanche rescue dogs in Colorado was never in Stone Keller's
plans—especially with Felicity Winslow, his best friend's sister. But after a
reckless motorcycle accident ruins his rodeo career, Felicity and the dogs
could be just what he needs to put the pieces of his life back together...

### A COWBOY TO RELY ON
*Wyoming Ranchers* • by Jill Kemerer
Still processing his grief, Jet Mayer is shocked to learn his late brother had
a secret wife and child. Caring for his sister-in-law, Holly Mayer, and infant
niece is a responsibility Jet's not sure he can handle. But could opening his
home to them be exactly what they all need?

### SEARCHING FOR HOME
by Jill Weatherholt
Heading home to recover from an injury, bull rider Luke Beckett plans to
keep to himself—until he comes face-to-face with his ex-girlfriend, physical
therapist Meg Brennan, and the triplets in her care. With Meg's troubled
little nephew reminding Luke of himself, helping out this makeshift family
might be just what the doctor ordered...

### HIS ROAD TO REDEMPTION
by Lisa Jordan
Battle-scarred veteran Micah Holland is trying to turn his life around. When
he inherits a farm, he discovers his co-owner is childhood frenemy
Paige Watson. Paige has her own plans for the place, which don't include
him. Can they set aside their differences and create a lasting legacy?

---

**LOOK FOR THESE AND OTHER LOVE INSPIRED BOOKS WHEREVER
BOOKS ARE SOLD, INCLUDING MOST BOOKSTORES, SUPERMARKETS,
DISCOUNT STORES AND DRUGSTORES.**

LICNM1221